To our beautiful Roy. ♡
From Nanna
(& Papa)

the writer of this book, Marty
is a good friend of Crystal Hogen
(I enjoyed it too.)

NIGHTMARE CLIFF
A Dreams West Series Book

Marty G Hogen
2013

PRESS

Dedication

To Ulian, Judah and Uriah. Ulian, may your choices always be true to your heart. Judah, may you always see through eyes of wonder. Uriah, may you always hunger and thirst for righteousness. My grandsons may you never lose your inquisitiveness. May your lives be filled with joy and bring glory to God.

Table of Contents

Prologue

Spring—the perfect time for a young boy's fancies to be filled with rocks and trees, frogs and ponds and all things wild and free. Spring—the master plan to help us forget the cold, bleak memories of winter past.

For Aaron Miller, spring was the season of new beginnings. Aaron was at that wonderful age in his life when each new spring he was a little bit taller, a little bit stronger and a little bit wiser. Each spring he found that what, just a year ago had been out of reach, was now within his grasp.

With the coming of spring new adventures beckoned to him promising even greater understanding of life's mysteries. It was as if the wind whispered, "Follow me. There are so many things I want to show you!" and Aaron was eager to see them all, adding them to the experiences he had already accumulated in his twelve years of life.

He really was quite knowledgeable and for him school held little interest. In fact, it was boring. It wasn't that Aaron wasn't eager to learn, he was, but he was quite sure that he had already learned everything there was to know, at least at school. And while he didn't know absolutely everything, he was confident he knew the lion's share of it. However, at twelve years old what you know and what you *think* you know can be worlds apart.

Aaron was sure about one thing, that nothing in the world could be more perfect than a boy and his dog sitting by a fishing hole; the warm sun on their faces, their toes digging into the dark moist earth, occasionally digging through a box of worms to find the biggest, fattest, juiciest bait. It just doesn't get any better than that. So why, when trouble by the name of Steven and Alicia came calling, was Aaron so eager to leave that perfection? Well now, if he had the answer to that question he wouldn't be in this horrible predicament, and there wouldn't be a story tell would there?

ONE

A small trickle of blood oozed down the side of the index finger of Aaron's right hand and the throbbing pain kept rapid time with the beat of his heart. The dark rich color of his own blood fascinated him and made it hard to concentrate. When did he cut his finger? He couldn't remember. He shook his head to clear his mind and realized he couldn't think about the pain or the blood. He needed to concentrate. He would be dead if he lost his grip on this rock, literally dead. It was at least a forty-foot drop from his ledge on the cliff to the rocky base.

Pain shot up his calf with the same intensity of cold water on a bad tooth. If he didn't move his hands to get a more solid grip on the rock his cramping feet would soon give out and slide off the narrow ledge keeping him from certain death.

"How did I get into this mess?" he moaned. He was furious with himself for letting Steven talk him into making this climb.

When they were standing at the bottom of the mammoth cliff gazing up, Aaron felt the size of an ant. Steven scrambled up so effortlessly that Aaron felt even smaller. To make matters worse Steven egged him on; "Ain't nothin' in the whole world as good as a swim after a rock climb."

It was the hottest day so far this spring and the creek that wound its way between Nightmare Cliff and Aaron's father's farm was already the principle topic of discussion. The way Steven talked climbing the cliff would be the most natural thing to do regardless of the fact that just a year ago Aaron wouldn't even have considered this stunt.

'I'm a year older,' Aaron thought, 'and Ma says I grew at least three inches last winter. Maybe I could climb this ol' cliff. It ain't so big anyway.'

His mind began to play tricks on him and the effect began to transform his physical stature to the size of his bravado. He could almost feel himself growing taller and stronger, if not wiser.

'Yeah, I bet I could climb this dumb ol' rock,' he convinced himself.

Steven nimbly dropped to the ground after his descent of the cliff and goaded Aaron by saying, "Even a baby could climb that thing. Course if yer scart' I'm sure Alicia'll understand. Some boys just ain't made fer' climbin' little rocks." Then he turned to Alicia and said, "Ya better not watch little Aaron here. He might embarrass hisself."

Alicia tried to hide her giggle, Steven laughed outright and Aaron's face turned red.

"This ain't nothin'!" Aaron said a little too loudly making his voice crack. Steven laughed harder and Alicia tried weakly to reassure Aaron.

"It's okay Aaron—yer just not as strong as Steven. Ya' don't have ta' prove nothin' ta' me," she giggled.

Aaron thought, "Why do girls always have ta' giggle? I'll bet she thinks I'm chicken."

Steven's voice broke the moment, "Come on. Let's just go swimmin'. I'm hot an' sweaty."

In an instant Aaron put his thoughts into action. He turned and stared straight up the cliff. It looked as though it went on forever but without flinching he leapt up toward the first hand hold.

Just minutes before he was at the bottom determined to succeed. Now he was in the middle of Nightmare Cliff, his strength had given out and it looked to Aaron like the only place to go was down, fast. 'This was crazy, why had he let Steven push him into this?' Steven was older, several inches taller, much stronger and better at rock climbing. In fact, Steven seemed to be better at everything and much more popular, particularly with girls.

A thought came to plague him, as if things could get worse. The real reason he was in this predicament was not Steven or even Alicia, it was his own foolish pride.

Aaron thought it very strange that less than a year ago he couldn't care less about girls but now, somehow, his opinion had changed. He found himself thinking more and more about them and wondering what they thought about him. Aaron knew that he didn't look like the older boys and that girls seemed to treat him differently then they treated boys like Steven. It was all very confusing to him but the harder he tried not to think about it the more the topic plagued him. He wanted to talk to Pa about it, but somehow, it just didn't seem right and besides, it was down-right embarrassing to admit you were thinking about girls.

"Is that why I'm hangin' on this cliff about to die, 'cause Alicia's standin' at the bottom?" the question flashed into his mind. He couldn't believe his life had sunk so low. There had to be more to it than that, but there he was, about to plummet to a gory, painful death just to prove to some girl, that he was worthy of her admiration. The sad part was that it wasn't the first time he'd made a fool of himself. Even sadder was that if he lived, it probably wouldn't be the last. It seemed that Steven could talk Aaron into anything in the name of friendship, a good time and now even for the favor of girls.

As a matter of fact, Aaron still wasn't out of the dog-house after the last stunt he had pulled under Steven's guiding hand, and it had seemed like such a good idea at the time.

TWO

*I*f there ever was a goody-two-shoes, it was Aaron's older sister, Mary. As far as Aaron could see Mary had never done anything wrong in her whole life, or at least nothing that she had ever been blamed for. But I guess with a younger brother like Aaron in the picture you didn't really need anyone else to blame. He managed to get into enough trouble for both of them. Maybe that is why, when Steven suggested a way to bring some imperfection into Mary's otherwise perfect little world, Aaron had thought it was a great idea, besides, it promised to be a lot of fun.

Mary always helped her mother with the wash on Mondays. It would usually take them the better part of a day to get all the clothes clean, hung on the line to dry and neatly folded. Aaron couldn't imagine a worse job but somehow Ma and Mary always had big smiles on their faces while they worked. They talked and laughed like they were actually having all kinds of fun.

Aaron had, what he considered, a real job helping his father either working in the field or down at the barn. In the field, the work was generally hard and always dirty but Aaron, like most boys, didn't mind getting dirty. It was traditionally a time when

Pa would use whatever they were doing as a tool to teach his son the importance of taking pride in his accomplishments. Pa Miller believed that it was his duty to make sure his children learned that every choice carries with it its own consequence. The general rule being, that if you make the right choices you will have desirable consequences. Pa was not blind to reality and he knew that life did not always follow this general rule of thumb but he also believed that more times than not it would prove true. While passing along this kind of information to your children is easy, insuring that they always remember the principle is, unfortunately, impossible.

Pa used to tell Aaron that the most important part of work was not *getting it done,* but rather, *getting it done right.* "If you don't have time to do something right the first time—how you ever gonna' find time to do it again?" Pa would ask?

Aaron couldn't quite figure out what one thing had to do with the other so one day Pa explained it like this, "Let's say we got a fence that needs mendin' but we're in a hurry so we do a *hurry up* job on it, you know, skimpin' on the wire, not stretchin' it tight cause the fence posts aren't strong enough ta hold the tension. What do ya' suppose'l happen?"

"I don't know," seemed like a safe answer for Aaron.

"Well son, let's think about it. What do cows like ta' do when they walk along a fence line?" Pa wasn't going to let Aaron get off quite that easily.

"Rub on it," came the simple answer from Aaron.

"And what happens when they start rubbin' on the fence and fence posts?" Pa pursued.

Aaron thought for a minute. The images of cattle, scattered in fields where they shouldn't be, came to mind. "They find the holes and the weak spots," Aaron responded, sure of his answer. "Then they climb through the fence an' get where they're not supposed to be, causin' all kinds a' trouble." He smiled finally sensing where his father was going with this lesson.

"That's exactly right son. Well, course then ya' have to stop what you're doin', chase animals back home and fix a fence that ya' already spent time fixin' once. See, if ya' don't take the time to do it right the first time, yer' probably gonna' have ta' make time to do it again."

Aaron thought that made sense, at least until his pa started talking about the apostle Paul and the Bible.

"The most important reason ta' always do your best is 'cause that's what Jesus wants you to do. The apostle Paul put it like this, 'It is good to be zealous all the time, not just when I am with you.'" Then he went on to explain to Aaron that zealous meant to do something eagerly with all your heart, not just half way.

Well, Aaron didn't really see what the apostle Paul had to do with anything and he sure didn't figure Paul was talking about fixing a broken fence post.

Aaron was always in favor of doing things, the short cut way, but Pa wouldn't budge from his principals. Of course, the short cut ways usually had more to do with getting done quicker than doing the job right. Honestly, Aaron couldn't see anything wrong with wanting to get the job done sooner so he could go to the creek to fish or swim or go hike up on the mountain.

For a young boy, there was nothing better than discovering the secrets of nature, like for instance, a honey comb hidden inside an old tree where bees had built their nest and spun a dripping sweet golden reward. Gosh, isn't that what boys are supposed to do on a hot spring afternoon?

Now don't get the wrong idea, Ma and Pa Miller didn't treat their children like slaves. In fact, they always made sure that the kids had plenty of time to do the things they wanted to, that is after they did their chores and helped out around the place. But every afternoon Pa would set aside free time so Mary and Aaron could be kids and do what kids like to do.

Mary just loved to stay home and help mom in the kitchen or the garden but no sooner was Aaron's work done then he would be off to see his friends and find out what adventure they would have that day. It was a good life and the Miller children learned that hard work had its rewards, not the least of which was that their Ma and pa appreciated what they did and that their efforts contributed to the well-being of the family.

One Monday they had a surprise. Pa said he and Ma had to go to town to pick up something at the train station. Going to town was usually a family trip so Mary and Aaron didn't quite know what to make of this.

Aaron and Pa would curry and brush the horses until their coats glistened, then they would harness the team and hook up the buckboard. One of Aaron's favorite things was when he got to drive part of the way to town. Ma and Mary would sit on the second seat dressed in their Sunday best clothes and bonnets. Pa and he slicked their hair down with grease, put on their going-to-church clothes and proudly drove their women-folk the three miles to town. Once they were there Ma and Mary would spend their time dreaming over fabric in the mercantile and Pa and Aaron would look at the latest farm equipment and listen to men swap stories at the blacksmith shop.

So when Mary and he heard that they couldn't go to town they were at first confused and then disappointed. Finally Pa said he and Ma were bringing home a big surprise and they would just have to wait and see what it was. He said that they were old enough to stay on their own and to see to all the chores themselves. That made Mary and Aaron feel grown up, special and trusted.

Ma and Pa left for town after putting Mary in charge, just because she was older. Pa said Aaron didn't have to do any work other than the daily chores so he thought his day was free and he began to conjure up the afternoon's adventures. Then Ma struck the mighty blow, "Aaron, you can help your sister with the washing," she informed him.

"Ah, Ma. Do I have ta? That's women's work. Men don't do that!" Well, of course, he protested loudly—but that was the wrong thing to say.

He looked to his pa for what he imagined would be support of his protest, but Pa just frowned and said it was only fair since Mary would be doing it by herself. Aaron pleaded with his pa, trying to convince him that it wasn't the kind of thing that a boy should be doing. After all it was Saturday and one of his friends might come to visit. What would he ever do if someone should see him up to his elbows in the laundry tub? Pa said it would do him good to see how hard his ma and Mary work and that it wouldn't hurt his hands to spend some time in soapy water. "Besides," he said, "it's good for us to do things we don't want to do. It builds our character."

He reminded Aaron that Jesus said we should always lend a hand where there was a need. Aaron thought to himself that he sure didn't remember any parables about scrubbin' britches, but no matter how vocal his protest, it was no use.

As Mary and he waved good-bye, the wagon slowly disappeared from sight. Aaron turned to address his task master and let her know that in no way did he intend to touch women's clothing. Mary, in her usual bossy way, said that if she had to touch his filthy things that he certainly wouldn't die from touching her clothes. And with that announcement she sauntered off to do her chores.

Aaron sat down in the middle of the dusty lane. His world had just come crashing down around him. He was instantly lost in a cavern of self-pity. He sat there moping, unable to pull himself out of his mournful attitude. Gradually he became aware of an insistent pressure on his back. The force became stronger and now was accompanied by a high pitched whistling sound. Then a cold wet nose pressed into the back of his neck.

"Beat it Sam, I'm not in the mood," he groused.

But Sam kept nudging and then put her paw on his arm. Aaron tried again to push her away but without success. Finally he gave in and lifted his left arm. That was all the invitation Sam ever needed. She pushed her soft head under Aaron's arm, lay down and rested her chin on his leg. She was content. Aaron found himself suddenly jealous of a dog's life.

Sam never complained about what they were doing as long as they were together. It didn't matter if they were hiking through the forest, swimming in the creek, sorting cattle, plowing a field, doing chores or yes, even doing the laundry. As long as she was with Aaron she didn't care. She was as faithful and steadfast as a dog could be, and definitely man's very best friend. Aaron thought that he certainly knew no other friendship that was as unconditional—no love as forgiving or as patient. Then, suddenly, a verse came to his mind. "There is a friend who is closer than a brother." Well, sure, Jesus was all of those things but Sam you could reach out and touch. Sam, a boy could smell and hear. Sam wasn't something invisible that you had to just believe in. Sam was always at the foot of the bed each morning and hers' was the last face he saw before he fell sleep at night. Aaron didn't have to have faith to believe in his dog. Sam always knew exactly what kind of mood he was in and responded accordingly. What other friend would do that?

Aaron sat and sulked for a while longer petting and stroking Sam's back. All the while Sam's eyes were fixed on him, expectantly, as if to say, "There's chores to be done." Finally Aaron looked at her, shrugged his shoulders and got up. After all, there was a cow to milk, horses to feed, pigs and goats to feed, a gate to fix and stalls that needed fresh straw. He was so full of his own misery that he hardly noticed the work he was doing.

Before he knew it the rumbling in his stomach reminded him that it must be getting close to dinner time. He took stock of the work that was left to do and realized he was nearly through. Just pigs and goats left to feed, including mean old Billy. Aaron was working in the grain bin mixing the pig mash when he noticed the hair on Sam's back stand up.

"What's the Matter girl," he asked. Suddenly a bang so loud that it made the walls of the granary vibrate, sent him to the floor. Instantly darkness covered him like a down quilt. He scrambled up through the loose grain trying to re-orient himself in the darkness. Finally, looking up and back, he realized that the door of the granary had swung shut.

The inside of a granary is not a pleasant place to be, even when there is ample light, but in the dark, the dusty smell, heat and close quarters could be particularly eerie and now the only illumination was from a tiny shaft of light, a golden ray that danced through the upper window. Particles of grain dust, suspended in the air, drifted upwards in the beam as if irresistibly drawn toward the hole in the roof. Sam was still facing the door her teeth barred now making a very intimidating growling sound—a sound she reserved for the most sinister situations. Something was outside the door of the granary!

Suddenly the vision of feathers, bones and blood in the chicken yard reminded Aaron of the bear that broke into the barnyard wreaking havoc a week ago. Pa had said it was probably just traveling through but if it had cubs it was very dangerous. Aaron wondered how he could ever defend himself with nowhere to run and no place to hide. He looked around in the dim light and finally spotted a broken shovel handle. As he picked it up he prayed harder and faster than he ever prayed before and his short life passed before his eyes.

Sure, he had done some mean things in his life but did he really deserve to end up bear food? A sinking feeling in the pit of his stomach added to his feeling of terror. Consumed by fear he froze. What else could he do? Slowly, he began to have rational thoughts again. He realized that if there was a bear and it came through the door of the granary he would be the first thing it saw. So he carefully and quietly moved to the wall and made himself as inconspicuous as possible. He waited and waited and waited. Then, without warning, the door flew open! Sam barked and growled baring her teeth and snarling and Aaron dropped the shovel handle, quailed against the wall and prepared to meet his maker.

THREE

*J*ust then, a taunting voice from below brought Aaron back
to the present and his precarious position on the cliff.

"What's a matter, ya too weak or just too chicken? Maybe
I should send Alicia ta' come up there an' help ya'," Steven
howled with laughter. "I knew ya' couldn't do it. Yer gonna'
have ta' stay up there all night. Hope the bears ain't too hungry
tonight."

Bears, why did that word have such a familiar ring? With
all his heart Aaron hated Steven; hated him for what he was,
but even more he hated himself for what he was not and he
hated Alicia for being a girl. Then he hated himself again for
ever thinking that what she thought of him was important. All
of a sudden he thought of Pa. He would be furious. He and
Ma had warned him time and time again about trying to be
something that he wasn't.

Aaron knew he couldn't hold on much longer so in shear
desperation he thrust his hands up and to the side hoping to
reach the shelf of rock the climbers called the Bear's Hug.
His left foot slipped but somehow the right foot stuck in a

small crack and his right hand shot just high enough for him to grasp the ledge. He hung on with all his might, in spite of the pain and blood, as he clawed the rock with his left hand hoping to gouge out a place for fingers to grip. For a moment success, then his right foot slipped and no longer could he hold his body's weight with just his hand. He had just enough time to scream a short desperate cry of help before falling down the rock, first slowly, then at a terrifying speed. His arms flailed wildly as the unforgiving rock ripped at clothes and flesh. He tried to grab hold of something—anything—but he was moving too rapidly. The giant, unforgiving mountain picked pieces of flesh off his body as he hurtled toward the base of the cliff. Rock ledges and outcroppings that he had labored to climb just minutes before passed in a blur of terrifying sights and sounds.

In the recess of our mind lies valuable information that can only be accessed by the proper stimulus. Terror is one such stimulus and that was just what Aaron needed to remember a tree root that had been a short refuge on his assent of this unrelenting nemesis. If only he could come close enough to catch it.

He prayed a quick desperate plea, "Lord, I'm too young ta die," and then, as if by a miracle, he caught a glimpse of the root below and by some trick of nature or his imagination, everything went into slow motion.

His body twisted around a boulder and he was just able to push with one foot and make a desperate lunge for the root! By the grace of God he grabbed it! He gripped it with strength that came solely from a source beyond him. Unfortunately the weight of his fall and the abruptness of his stop ripped his shoulder out of socket and slammed his head into the unfor-giving rock. In an instant of time a wave of nausea flooded over him and his vision blurred—tears pouring down his cheeks. He managed to turn his head just in time as his lunch made a surprise visit.

FOUR

*T*he door of the granary flew open and Aaron prepared to be eaten alive. A deep menacing, "Growl!" The gut wrenching noise echoed through the granary with an unnatural shriek! But somehow it seemed wrong. The pitch was too high and not like any bear Aaron had ever heard. It sounded altogether too human. Abruptly the granary echoed with loud mocking laughter.

"Did ya think it was a bear?" came an all too familiar voice.

"I know that voice," Aaron realized.

Suddenly Steven's smug rude face appeared and as quickly disappeared. He was up to his old tricks. Aaron stumbled to the granary door and bounded over the threshold. Outside the door Steven was rolling on the ground reveling over his little joke and Aaron's discomfort. Aaron's face must have turned three shades of red from embarrassment then the blood drained from it as the anger welled up inside him. He quickly grabbed the grain buckets and pushed passed the prankster.

"I knew it was you," Aaron lied. "Din't scare me at all. Ya had ol' Sam goin' though."

"Ya were too, scar't," Steven teased. "You should see yer face, it's white as yer sister's petticoats hangin' on the line. Better check yer drawers, ya' might wanta' freshin' up a bit," he taunted.

The washing! The reason for his misery all came flooding back to Aaron's mind. Mary had obviously started the laundry without him. He knew he was going to be in big trouble if he didn't finish his chores and give her a hand. The dilemma must have showed on his face because Steven's merriment over his joke was cut short."What's a matter with you?" he asked? "Ya look like it's the end of the world."

Before Aaron had time to think better of it his mouth was in action. "I'm s'posed ta help sis with the wash. Ma an' Pa went ta' town 'n left Mary in charge and she's bossin' me like nobody's business," he blurted out.

"Well, if yer ma an' pa ain't here there's no need yer stickin' round. Let's go," Steven advised with his usual air of authority.

"Na, I can't," Aaron moaned."

"Oh if yer scare't a yer big sister, I best be goin'," he mocked.

"I ain't scared a' her, but what am I s'posed ta' do Steven?" Aaron asked. For a moment he saw what looked like a twinkle in Steven's eye.

Then the older boy pulled Aaron close and said, "Ya wanta' play a trick on 'er? Show 'er whose the real boss? It'd be lots' a fun," he goaded.

"I don't know Steven. I don't want ta' get inta trouble."

"Don't worry," he said as he pulled Aaron into the granary. "You won't get in any trouble. Here's what we do."

25

FIVE

*M*ary was just pulling a load of clothes out of the rinse tub as Aaron came through the kitchen door onto the back porch. She glanced at him with a look much louder than words. "Where have you been?" she quizzed. She immediately put her hands on her hips and glared intently. Aaron shook his head and squinted, his heart sped up momentarily. When had Ma returned? He hadn't heard the buggy come into the yard. He rubbed his eyes twice before he realized it was, in fact, Mary who stood in front of him, but her attitude, the set of her jaw, the way her lips pursed together, even her hair was pulled together in a tight bun the way Ma's always was. And that one long strand of dark brown hair that never seemed to stay ensnared by the hair combs was streaming down the left side of her face. It was uncanny. He was sure that if he blinked hard Ma would be standing in front of him expectantly awaiting his answer.

"I, uh, I was just feeding the goats and uh, uh—I think something's wrong with Heidi. You better come see." The weaving of the web had begun, suddenly all doubts about this being the right thing to do left Aaron's mind. How dare Mary look so much like Ma. The fact that his sister had been left in charge heaped burning coals on the tinder of his ego. The trap was set and for the first time this morning Aaron's heart felt glad.

Mary immediately registered concern. Heidi was her prize doe goat. She really was a beautiful creature with long droopy ears and patches of alternating chocolate brown and tan coloring on her back and sides.

"What's wrong with her," Mary asked? "Is she sick or hurt or what?"

"I don't know? You better come see," he said with all the sincerity he could muster.

Mary immediately dropped her load of laundry back in the rinse tub, tucked the back of her skirt into her front waistband so she could run and followed him to the goat barn.

The goat barn was actually a low lean-to that butted up to the barn. In front of the lean-to was a series of pens and corrals made of board fencing. Through a series of chutes and alleys you could actually herd a small flock of animals around the barn, across the lane, through the garden and into the yard that surrounded the Miller home. Sometimes in the fall they would let the sheep or goats into the garden and yard to eat the remaining cornstalks and garden refuse.

Now it just so happened that the buck goat, Billy, was being kept in a pen closest to the garden and subsequently the yard. Unbeknownst to Mary, Steven had led Billy through the chutes and alleys so that he was just one gate away from the yard. Mary's freshly cleaned laundry waved an invitation to the big buck goat from Ma's clothesline. As previously arranged, Steven quietly waited to open the remaining silent wooden sentry and usher Billy into the yard.

It has been said that goats, and especially buck goats named Billy, will eat anything. While that is not exactly true, it is true that a goat's primary instinct, not unlike a little baby, is to taste everything. Steven and Aaron's intention was for Mary to be startled and maybe a little frightened by the presence of Billy. Mary loved goats in general and her Heidi in particular but she was deathly afraid of the big buck goat.

One time, years ago, when she was alone in the goat pen, Billy had reacted rather aggressively towards her and his large curled horns and rather foul smell had sent her into hysterics. Ever since then she had steered clear of all of the males, even while they were young. Billy really wasn't dangerous but he could be somewhat obstinate when he had his mind set on something.

Aaron purposely opened the gate and let Mary enter the pen first. He knew she would be intent on Heidi long enough to give the signal to Steven to turn Billy loose in the yard. "Heidi, what's the matter girl?" Mary said softly. "Are you okay?" Heidi pulled her head out of the hay feeder and looked at Mary. She had a stem of alfalfa hanging out of her mouth and an expression on her face that said, "Excuse me, I'm eating." Heidi walked over to Mary and sniffed her hands and pockets. Satisfied that Mary wasn't hiding a special treat she walked back to the feeder and stuck her head back through the feeder slot. Mary walked slowly toward the feeder then stopped short.

"What's going on?" she said and wheeled around to give Aaron that look again. "Heidi's not sick is she? What are you trying to pull Aaron? So help me, I'll tell Ma an' Pa if this is another one of yer tricks."

"She was sick," he said, a little too fast and loud so that his voice cracked! "Or at least I thought she was. When I came in to feed she was lyin' in the corner of the shed an' she wouldn't get up, so I ran up and got you."

"You saw Heidi lying in the shed an' you came to the house to get me, is that what you said?" Mary questioned.

"Yeah, I told ya."

"Then how come the feeder is full of hay?" she asked.

"Danger! Be very careful!" Aaron's instincts told him. "Well, I meant I put hay in the feeder first and when Heidi didn't come ta eat I looked in the shed an' there she was. She's yer goat. Don't ya' even care if she's sick or not? I thought you'd be glad that I came ta get ya. I can't help if she's okay now. Some thanks I get fer tryin' to do the right thing." Aaron stormed off towards the gate hoping he had sufficiently distracted Mary from her cross examination. To his surprise she came running after him, grabbed his arm and hugged him.

"Oh Aaron, I'm so sorry. I just love Heidi so much I guess I got too excited. I should have thanked you for taking notice of her and instead I didn't trust you. Aaron, you're a good brother. You've done a good job with all the chores by yourself, and the gate ya' fixed looks good too. Can you forgive me? I guess I was mad because Ma an' Pa went ta town without us. But I shouldn't have taken it out on you. I'll tell ya' what. I know how ya' hate havin' ta do the wash, so I'll finish it myself. Why don't ya' go find Steven an' do somethin' fun?" Mary gushed!

Aaron's heart sank! It wasn't supposed to happen this way. Sisters aren't supposed to be nice and do generous things. For a fleeting second he saw an image in his mind of Billy the goat with the sleeve of Pa's best shirt hanging out of his mouth.

Aaron panicked, he had to do something and fast. Mary let go, smiled at him like he was an angel and started toward the gate. 'She didn't deserve this,' he thought.

"Oh God, I' m sorry. Help!" he breathed a short prayer. Before he knew what had happened he screamed, "Mary!" She jumped and turned to look.

"What is it Aaron? What's wrong?" She crossed back to him, "Aaron, are you okay? Ya' look like ya seen a bear."

Frantically he looked around wondering how to get out of this and then it came to him. "Where's Billy? I don't see Billy." He ran to the fence that bordered on Billy's pen and climbed halfway up. "Oh no, the gates open."

Mary questioned, "How could you see that far from here? What's going on Aaron?" suspicion clouding her voice once again.

"He's not in his pen Mary, the gates open! That's all I know." Aaron jumped over the fence and yelled, "I'm goin' ta' find Billy. If he's in the garden, we're in big trouble." At this point Mary headed back through the goat pen. If he could just beat her to the house maybe the damage could be kept to a minimum. He ran through each pen and gate as fast as he could. When he reached the gate that bordered on the garden he barely slowed down. Knowing it would be unlatched, since Steven had just taken Billy through it, he put his shoulder down and hit the gate fully expecting it to fly open leaving only the garden between him and the yard. The gate screamed against the latch but did not budge. Pain exploded in Aaron's shoulder as he bounced off the gate into the fence and landed face down in the manure!

SIX

*A*fter what seemed like hours Aaron was able to see some-thing other than stars. His whole side felt like it was on fire, his hand was covered with blood and his shoulder seemed to be going the wrong direction. Slowly he began to survey the immediate surroundings. For the moment he seemed to be in no imminent danger of sliding any farther down the cliff. The tree that belonged to the root that had miraculously presented itself to him had been cut down long ago. By the size of the roots he could see the tree must have been huge. The roots wound themselves in and around the rock of the cliff, ironically known as, Nightmare Cliff.

Aaron remembered his pa saying that when his pa was a boy, there had been a large land slide that exposed this rock face, and boys had been climbing it ever since. So, by the random events of nature, he had been saved by a tree that used to be at the top of the cliff on flat ground. At that moment something in Aaron told him that it was the hand of God that kept him from falling to an excruciating death and the concept of a guardian angel took one step closer to reality. After saying a quick *'thanks'* he twisted gently to the left to relieve some of the pressure on his head which was still smashed against the rock. Pain seared through his shoulder. Again a wave of nausea convulsed his body. He reached with his left hand to touch his shoulder and the hand came away with bits of blood smeared cloth. He then touched his face and felt the same warm sticky dampness.

By the grace of God, he was alive, but it seemed just barely. His only earthly hope, Steven, was at the base of the cliff. Aaron tried to call to him but very little sound came out of his mouth. He managed to move just enough to look over his shoulder to the foot of the cliff. Steven and Alicia were nowhere to be seen. They wouldn't have deserted him—or would they? No sound came from below and painfully it began to sink in just what kind of friends they were. Then Aaron tried to force himself not to think that way. "No! They had been so terrified by the fall, that immediately they ran for help—that's it. Sure that's what happened," he thought.

"Yeah, that had ta' be it," he tried to reassure himself, but with little success. Well, he had survived the fall that much was certain. Turning his head back toward the cliff he could still see the crimson stains he made tumbling down the rock. Then his eye caught something that looked out of place in the jagged rock. It was grayish white and smooth and round. Tenderly he moved his left hand up high enough to touch the anomaly that was dislodged by the fall. It felt porous but smooth, like a piece of wood. There was familiarity in this object but not enough to place it. Suddenly it came to him, the bone yard on the farm—definitely it was bone. With renewed effort Aaron pulled and more of the treasure became exposed and he began to see and recognize the shape. Pulling a little harder, momentarily oblivious to the situation, pain or surroundings, the object came out of the rock and dirt that had been its grave for who knows how long. A perfectly formed human skull fell into the young boy's hand. He screamed and shrank against the rock sanctuary. There, in his hand, rested the remains of what had once been a living head. He twisted hard, away from the horror, and the motion tore at the dislocated shoulder sending a jolt of pain down through his chest. The world began to turn violently on its axis, his vision narrowed and all went black.

SEVEN

*D*azed, his shoulder aching, Aaron slowly began to turn over. As he put pressure on his arm trying to force himself off the ground, the pain caused him to cry out and the sharp burning reminder of the unyielding gate sliced down his back. His eyes felt like they were rolling around in his head as he lay back in the manure and caught his breath. Then, like a nagging tooth ache, the memory of his sister and the washing and Billy returned.

Billy! Oh no, where was Billy? He had to get to the yard before Mary. He forced himself to sit up and then to stand gripping the fence. The pain was dizzying but he had to get through the gate, cross the garden and retrieve Billy from the yard before the goat did any damage. Slowly unlatching the gate and stumbling across the garden he hurried to the gate on the house end of the garden, checked to see that it was unlatched before going through it and rushed into the yard.

Mother's yard was always a beautiful sight to behold. Along each fence were rows of gorgeous flowers. On the end of the house near the vegetable garden was a large circle of prize-winning roses. Between the back porch which contained the summer kitchen and the flowers along the fence, were long rows of clothes lines. The two women spent hours weeding, feeding and pruning their pride and joy, making sure the masterpiece of gardening looked just right. Every year Ma and Mary would enter her roses in the county fair and she always brought home the purple ribbon. The garden work was just one of the many everyday tasks that Ma used to instill, in Mary, a sense of pride in her work. She used to tell her that everything on the earth was from God for us to enjoy and the best way to find enjoyment in it was to treat it like it's a gift from your very best friend. Then she would quote the first verse of Psalm 19, "The heavens declare the glory of God; the skies proclaim the work of His hands."

Aaron entered the yard and stopped short. Something was different. Ma's roses! They looked like someone had come through with a long bladed scythe and removed everything over a certain level. There were flowers on the ground around the bushes where Billy had spit them out after deciding that roses weren't as good to eat as they looked, but the goat was nowhere to be seen. Aaron quickly moved toward the backyard, the pain in his shoulder reminding him of the recent collision with the gate. As he rounded the corner he caught sight of Billy's back side. The way his legs were straining indicated that the goat was struggling to back up but his head was behind a sheet and Aaron couldn't see the source of resistance. Another two steps and Billy's head emerged.

Few things in this world are as deliciously entertaining as a white petticoat suspended in midair with a large buck goat on one end and a determined young girl pulling on the other.

Under any other circumstances Aaron would have burst into laughter at the spectacle, but at this moment in time it struck fear in his heart. First sight of Mary and the determination with which she pulled on the cloth convinced him that her anger at the destruction of the garden had overpowered any anxiety she might still have of Billy. In between struggling and shouting she kicked at the obstinate goat who must have been quite amused at the game Mary was playing. Billy would pull back and then sideways shaking the cloth like a dog with a rag. Then, unannounced, he released his grip on the petticoat in his mouth, apparently tired of the game, and Mary plopped hard on to the ground with the cloth as her prize. Billy must have decided he'd had enough fun for one day. He trotted over to the flowers by the fence to investigate the possibility of an after play snack. At just that time Sam came in the yard, spotted an animal out of place and proceeded to go to work setting things to rights.

In a flurry of hair, dust and barking, Sam chased Billy back where he belonged. All this had taken place in seconds. Aaron stood dazed by what he had witnessed, still reeling from the encounter with the non-moving gate. Gradually the magnitude of the disastrous surroundings began to register.

On the ground, surrounded by soiled shirts, sheets and pants Mary sat crying. Her face was covered by the petticoat Billy had decided wasn't worth eating. Ma and Mary's flowers were trampled and eaten, laundry was strewn all around and the summer kitchen was covered in pellets of a not so tidy visitor. Aaron's shoulder throbbed as he sat down in the grass, alligator tears filling his eyes. Had someone walked into the yard at that moment they could easily have thought a tornado had just touched down wreaked havoc and then departed.

When Mary finally climbed out from under the cloth covering her she was no longer crying. She had a look on her face that could melt an iceberg. She glared at her brother accusingly. "What have you done? What have you done, Aaron? The laundry is a mess and look at Ma's flowers!" She was up by this time, marching through the destruction enumerating the crimes one by one. "You're going to pay for this mischief. Just wait till Pa gets home." At that moment Sam's barking invaded their thoughts. This time, however, it was a welcoming bark that could only mean one thing, Ma and Pa were back!

Aaron quickly jumped to his feet looking frantically around. What should he do? Could he set things right? No, not in a lifetime. The next thought came quickly. Where could he hide, no hole was deep enough, no cave dark enough. In a flash he imagined years of loneliness with no place to call home and no family. No! Running away was not the answer. Sitting back down in the midst of the disarray, his head sank to his lap as he steeled himself, preparing for his fate. It was then that he noticed Mary had not moved. She was simply standing in the middle of torn and dirty laundry staring straight at him with a big devilish smile on her face. Aaron's life passed quickly before his eyes.

EIGHT

*J*eremiah and Ruth Miller lived a life of no compromise. They stood fast, first, on the Word of God and second, on the value of their family. Jeremiah was an elder in the small church they attended and to him it was his life, not just a church assignment. People would come from miles around to get his prayers and advice on all kinds of important issues. His counsel always came straight from his heart and was spoken in love which had been formed by the Word of God. He chose to believe that the Bible was the true and complete word of God. He was not inclined to accept certain parts and reject others but rather he believed it all, yet his was not a faith based on legalism or religion. He had come to know, through his study of the Word of God and his fervent prayer life, that Jesus was a personal God who wanted a relationship with each and every one of His children. He also knew, from the Bible that God's desire is that all should be saved and none should perish.

Jeremiah believed in the great commission but he didn't consider himself a preacher. He believed that the best way to tell someone about Jesus was to show them God's love.

Instead of preaching the gospel of Christ through words, he lived it. It was interesting that everyone knew Jeremiah was a Christian but few people had actually heard him quoting the Bible, even though he was responsible for leading numerous people to the Lord. He always tried, as best he could, to live his life as an example to those with whom he came in contact.

Ruth Miller, Jeremiah's wife, was a Proverbs 31 woman. She thought first of God and secondly of her family. She never put herself first but always made sure that her family had what they needed, not only to live but to grow in their love of God, thirst for wisdom and generosity of heart. She was a woman of genuine beauty, the kind that comes from inside. She was never willing to just do for her children; rather she insisted that they learn all that she knew and more. She encouraged them to do the best they could in all that they did. It was through her teaching that Mary and Aaron learned how to live to please God. She showed them, through the way she lived her life, how to give back to God all He had given them. As Jeremiah loved her, she loved him. There was never a question in her mind whether she had married the right man and it was to those steadfast truths that she held so dearly.

Jeremiah was not perfect and never would be. He had made many mistakes in his life and he didn't try to hide them, in fact he was always willing to expose them if it would help others avoid the same pitfalls. It was his generous nature and servant heart that endeared him to all he came in contact with and it was those character traits that his wife loved so much.

While they had both made mistakes as they raised their family, they did the best that they could and didn't use those mistakes as excuses. Their children were not perfect, God only knows, but they too were made in God's image. Jeremiah and Ruth knew that God had given them a measure of wisdom to make the best decisions they could and when they stumbled He would pick them up, brush them off and set them on the right path once again.

Then came the horrific news that Jeremiah's younger brother, Peter and his wife Marie had been killed in a terrible barn fire. When the truth finally sank in they became numb and perplexed. How could such a tragedy be God's will? Where was He in all of this? What good could come from such disaster? Peter was still a young man and had been married only a little more than three years. He and Marie, had a little two year old boy, Isaiah, who had survived the fire even though he was badly burned and the question now was: what would happen to him? Since the fire, Isaiah had made a remarkable recovery physically and seemed ready to leave the care of the doctor. But where would he go?

Jeremiah's sister Joanna and her husband Jonathan lived near Peter and Marie and they were very close to them but Joanna and Jonathan already had twelve children of their own and while they were willing it would be an undue burden to expect them to take in one more boy, especially one so frail and young as Isaiah. He would need full time attention and costly medicine until he was completely healed from his burns.

The more Ruth and Jeremiah prayed about what to do the more convinced they became that the logical thing was to take the boy into their home no matter what the cost to the family. As God revealed this plan to them, they began to see it as an answer to their own prayers.

After Aaron was born, Ruth had become very sick. The doctors had counseled her and her husband that to have more children would be at the risk of her very life. This realization had been a source of constant pain for Ruth, as she blamed herself for her inability to have more children. She knew Jeremiah had always wanted a large family. In fact, Ruth and Jeremiah both had dreamed of the large family they would have and how, with that family, they would move west to the frontier seeking God's blessing on their adventure and new life. When the revelation sank in that they would have no more children, they traveled through the wilderness journey of that disappointment by the strength of God alone. The Holy Spirit showed them that they must accept the fact but continue to believe God for healing and further provision for their family. Jeremiah had willingly set aside his dreams of the *wild west* and settled down to be the best that he could be, right where he was, for his Lord and Savior and for his family.

Now, in this tragedy, it seemed that God was using for good what the enemy had intended for bad. Here, in this small child, was an answer to prayer for another son. In God's infinite wisdom, He had determined to give them a son who would cause them to rely, even more whole heartedly, on the single source of their provision, God Himself.

They embraced this peculiar answer to prayer and asked that God would guide them in every step. Jeremiah bought the train tickets for young Isaiah to be brought to Strasburg to become the newest member of the Miller family. Ruth and Jeremiah were determined to love and nurture Isaiah as if he were their very own flesh and blood. They were convinced that

God's blessing would accompany the child as he traveled the one hundred and fifty miles to his new home.

As Jeremiah and Ruth rode toward the train station, they were both unusually quiet. They traveled for a couple miles before Ruth broke the silence,

"Did I ever tell you I love you Jeremiah Miller?"

"Maybe once, I don't remember." Jeremiah joked.

Ruth grinned at his response. Love was not just an assumed emotion in the Miller house hold; it was something that both Jeremiah and Ruth knew was very important to say as well as to live. Ruth moved a little closer to Jeremiah, took his arm and laid her head on his shoulder, "Well, it's true you know." she reassured him.

He tilted his head and rested it on top of hers, "Yes, that's one thing I'm very sure of." They rode along in the wagon this way for a short distance when he asked her, "Are you ready to be a mother again?"

"I think so." she responded. "One thing's for sure this is the shortest and easiest delivery I've ever had." They both laughed as Jeremiah slapped the reigns and urged the horses on a little faster.

Jeremiah and Ruth knew the long train trip and bumpy wagon ride to their small farm would be very hard on the traumatized Isaiah. They had prepared a very soft bed in the back of the wagon for Isaiah to lie on and they prayed that God would give him the strength to make the journey none the worse for wear.

They had heard reports from Joanna of the young child's condition, so they were prepared for the worst but the sight that assaulted them when they arrived at the train station was more than Ruth could bear. Before her eyes stood a very young child whose face and arms were covered with evidence of the tremendous heat that scared his physical appearance. But what gripped Ruth the most was the look in Isaiah's eyes. They were fixed on something, it was impossible to tell what, but they rarely blinked. Behind his stare you could almost see the confusion in his mind as the vision of the fire seemed to replay itself over and over again.

What the Millers had not been told was that since the fire, Isaiah had not made a sound and his mouth seemed to be frozen in a perpetual gasp of unbelief. Ruth broke into tears when she saw the shell of this tortured child. She went to him immediately and wrapped her arms around him. She hugged him to her breast and rocked him gently. He made no response but he did not pull away. It was if she were not even there. Jeremiah just stared and wondered at what moments ago they had considered a mighty blessing from God. His heart knew, at once, the work that lay ahead of his little family. This was a life that had been stolen by the enemy and he knew that only God could redeem it. He sank to his knees, calling on the name of Jesus, as he placed his hands gently on the little damaged soul and Ruth.

NINE

*A*aron couldn't stop the tears that streamed down his face. He was convinced that life as he knew it was over. He knew that his father was not a mean man but he also knew that he believed very strongly in discipline and had no problem applying forceful persuasion to a person's backside if he felt the consequences of the action warranted. Even more painful for Aaron, was the overwhelming realization that he had let his father down. He knew that his pa had confidence in him and trusted that he was responsible enough to follow through with the simple directives he had been given.

Peculiar in a boy's transformation to manhood are the watermarks that are visible along the shore of his emotional journey. Like the tide, they ebb and flow evidencing highs and lows. The highs can easily be recognized by the confident assurance exhibited in a young man's decision making process. The lows, however, often reveal themselves through doubt and confusion. Regardless of the quality of a father's parenting skills, he is the most dominant influence on the course his son's life will take. Therefore, often times what a father is, his son will be. Of course, there are exceptions to this rule, but to a great degree, it is true.

Jeremiah Miller and his son were a perfect example of this age old axiom for Aaron loved his father and wanted, more than anything, to please him. The curious thing was that, although Jeremiah had such a strong influence, Aaron found it easier to do exactly the opposite of what he knew he should do. In fact, he nearly always found himself, particularly when under the influence of Steven, doing what he knew he should not.

Jeremiah sensed the confusion Aaron was experiencing so one day he shared with him the dilemma of the apostle Paul who said that what he knew he should do, he could not, but that which he shouldn't do always came easy for him. He reassured Aaron that he could win the fight if he would just continue to bring all his concerns to Jesus, who in turn would take them to His Father. He said, "God wants us to be pure as He is pure, but we can't do that by ourselves. Only God can do it through us as He transforms our mind when we are born again." Jeremiah went on to teach that Galatians 5:16 states clearly that if we walk in the Holy Spirit we no longer have to be under the control of our selfish desires.

As much as Aaron understood what Pa told him, he still struggled with the temptations of the world around him and those temptations were always magnified with Steven in the picture. Steven was his best friend. Actually he was the only other boy who lived within 5 miles of the Miller farm. There was Alicia, but she was a girl and after all, what did girls know about having fun?

So now, once more, Aaron had messed up in such a way that he was sure the best thing would be for him to pack a small bag of essentials and hit the road. It was obvious to him that the Miller family would be far better off without him. He began to consider the various places that he might be able to go and start a new life. Somewhere in the back of his mind he remembered stories about young boys who worked for the railroad crews, carrying water to the men, serving lunch and doing other odd chores to help out. He'd heard that a boy could earn a dime a week if he worked really hard and didn't eat too much. Aaron began to wonder how much a dime a week was and whether it was enough to survive on when Nellie, the lead horse, came into sight quickly followed by Ma and Pa in the wagon. Too late!

TEN

Golden light painted the surrounding trees as a gentle breeze played at the edges of the rock and dirt cradling the injured young rock climber high above the safety of grass and solid footing. A large honey bee worked diligently at the blossoms of a hanging vine next to Aaron's head and for just a brief moment it mistook his nose for a safe landing site.

The young adventurer stretched, yawned and snuggled a little deeper in his warm covers but the enticing smell of Ma's hotcakes began to stir his senses. Slowly the thought of Pa out doing chores by himself invaded his peaceful repose. Then a sound, first miles away but quickly coming closer, penetrated his comfort. What could be making such a strange noise?
"I don't want to get up yet, I'm so tired Pa, can't I sleep just a little longer?" he mumbled. The buzzing refused to go away so Aaron opened his eyes, "Pa stop buzzin' at me. I'll get up, I promise."

Disturbed by the movement of its new landing site, the honey bee buzzed a little louder, made contact with its stinger for emphasis, and flew away. Aaron opened his eyes just in time to see a large bee applying its stinger to his nose. Through the blurred vision of his crossed eyes, the size of the bee doubled. Momentarily, all other pain disappeared as Aaron hollered and swatted, but when he did so, his foot shot out from under him and he slipped a short ways down the rock face. He instinctively grabbed for something to stop his fall. Both feet slid to a narrow ledge wide enough for him to feel more secure than he had since he began falling. His left hand still held tightly to the human skull and once again his focus shifted to the reminder of death at his fingertips.

Was this to be his fate? Would his bones wind up tucked into a crevice of this cliff, just as the skull in his hands had? Did anyone know where he was? Steven! Where were Steven and Alicia? Would they bring help or would they deny any knowledge of his whereabouts? Other than Sam, no one else knew where he was and the sun had almost set. He could just see the last rays pouring through the leaves of the big oak tree just above the top of the cliff. What if he had to spend the night here? Would he be able to hold on or would he slip off in the middle of the night? What would become of his remains lying at the foot of the cliff? Would he soon be reduced to bear food? If he fell to the bottom of the cliff would his body be eaten and then carried off to a place that no one would ever discover?

Now Aaron's nose began to throb, in rhythm to the pain in his head and shoulder. "Well, God, I suppose I deserve ta' die this way after all I've done lately. I don't figure you could ever forgive me fer the shear meanness in me." Aaron had never spoken so frankly to God before. "I don't expect ya' ta' save me, but I want ta' say I'm sorry anyways'. I been just plumb nasty ta' Mary. She gets real bossy but she's just bein' a girl.

I don't suppose she can help it any more an' I can help the meanness in me. So, God, I'm sorry." The more Aaron poured out his heart the more he found to say. "I wanted ta' be better, I really did, but ya' know how tough it is when yer just a boy." His thoughts returned to his two friends. "An' God, don't go so hard on Steven an' Alicia. They must be pretty near scarred ta' death over this." Feeling like he had made his peace with his Maker he resigned himself to the end. "I guess I'm ready fer ya' ta' take me now, if that's what ya' figure ya' need ta' do, an' I don't blame ya' fer doin' what ya' gotta do. I'm sorry I ain't better. Ma an' Pa'll probably be better off not ta' have ta' always be scoldin' me anymore."

Aaron had never prayed such a long or heart felt prayer in his life and somehow, afterwards, he felt better, even peaceful. By this time all traces of the sun were gone and the blanket of darkness was quickly smothering everything. The displaced skull somehow comforted Aaron. He thought, 'It's good to have someone to talk to, even if he don't have much to say.'

With the last moments of light, Aaron surveyed his precarious sanctuary. He found that the shelf of rock he was on was wider than he had first thought. In fact there was ample room to sit down. He slowly and carefully maneuvered his back against the wall of rock and his feet onto a small ridge that rose between him and the shear rise of the cliff. He braced his feet against the front of the ledge and made himself as comfortable as a young boy spending the night on the side of a cliff could.

ELEVEN

*L*ittle Isaiah slept fitfully on the long ride from the train station to the Miller farm. He would doze for a time and then wake with a start, as if being shaken. His face looked as if he wanted to cry or scream but no sound ever came from his mouth. Sitting in the rear of the wagon Ruth held him for the better part of the journey while Jeremiah urged the horses on. All the while he prayed, 'Lord, I know we have been selfish in our prayers. We have spent so much time telling you what we want and need and we forgot that the main point of prayer is to get to know You. Forgive us and help us come closer in our relationship with You. Father, I lay at your feet all my desires. I have asked You so many times to move us west and to help us establish a new life but now I know that You have a mission for us here. Show us how to help this little soul who has experienced more terror than anyone should ever have to face. Lord, I know that Your plan is perfect and I do not doubt Your will. With You I know we will have the strength to make it through this challenge.'

Ruth came quietly up to the seat of the wagon.

"Is he asleep?" Jeremiah whispered.

"For now." Ruth answered, without taking her eyes off of Isaiah. "How do things like this happen in God's kingdom?"

Jeremiah said, "Remember, Satan is still alive and well here on earth."

"Well I hate Satan!" Ruth breathed through clenched teeth.

Jeremiah had never known his wife to hate anything before. He was taken aback, yet felt the same way himself.

"What Satan has intended for evil, God will use for good." Jeremiah quoted.

"I know," Ruth replied, "but to see this child in such constant horror—it breaks my heart Jeremiah. How can he ever be healed?"

Jeremiah felt the frustration and pain Ruth was experiencing and started to respond with a bible verse, then something made him stop. Over the course of time, experience taught him that sometimes it is best to sit quietly and listen rather than try to solve every problem. He felt confident that this was one of those moments since Ruth knew all the appropriate verses for this situation, maybe better than he did. He decided to change the subject.

"How do you think Mary and Aaron are going to take this? Maybe we should have told them so they could have been a little better prepared."

"How could children be prepared for something like this?" Ruth shot back, a little too forcefully.

Jeremiah began to see that the consequences of their decision to take Isaiah into their home were much more far reaching than he ever dreamed. Since he first saw Isaiah on the train station platform, he hadn't even thought about the kids, let alone what their reaction might be. Now he became concerned about the burden the whole family would bear during the lengthy healing process they faced. Little did he know what lay ahead.

Lost in thought, he stared at the scenery that passed without any real recognition of where he was; tree blended into tree, rock walls appeared and faded into meadows that melted into cultivated fields which blurred into the verdant foliage of the hillsides. A growing tension in his fingers slowly overpowered the visual senses that he had allowed to soothe him. With the whinny of Nellie, the lead horse, reality streamed back full force.

"We're almost home." he said, more to himself than to Ruth. He looked over at the empty seat beside him, surprised that he hadn't even noticed when Ruth had climbed to the back of the wagon. He caught her eye as she looked up at him from where she was holding Isaiah, "It's going to be okay."

She smiled her first smile in hours, "uh, huh." she agreed and added "God is still in control, isn't He?"

He nodded and said, "More than ever." They both looked lovingly at Isaiah, Jeremiah smiled and gave the reigns a flick, "Git up there Nellie, old girl. Let's go home."

TWELVE

$\mathcal{A}$aron closed his eyes for a little while and determined to try to sleep. He was plenty tired enough and he figured that if he was going to slip off the side of the cliff, he would rather not be awake for it. The breeze picked up a little, blowing across the face of the cliff. What had been a refreshing relief in the heat of the day now caused an involuntary shiver to go through his body.

"It's gettin' cold." Aaron thought as he wrapped his arms around himself. The action caused his shoulder to throb with renewed vigor and he winced in pain. Sleep was out of the question while the pain was so intense. He began to feel sorry for himself once again, his eyes filled with tears and the lights in the distance danced crazily.

Lights, in the distance? 'Must be angels of death comin' for me,' he thought. He wondered if they could see him or just instinctively knew where death was about to happen. "They sure don't waste any time. You'd think they'd let a guy die first. Well, I guess I'm in no position ta' complain," he said to the skull. Aaron was fascinated by the lights bobbing and weaving in the dark. They looked like fireflies floating around; first going this way then that way, back and forth, coming towards him, now moving away, seemingly unsure of their ultimate destination. "They don't seem too smart for angels. Maybe they send fallen' angels fer somebody like me?" Aaron debated whether to try to call out to them in order to give them some direction, but then he decided if they were comin' to escort him to his death, he wasn't in any hurry. They could just find him on their own. No sense hurrying things any faster than they had to go, after all, he was just a young boy and it was sad enough that he had to finish his life in such an untimely way. He decided to let the lights find their own way. He closed his eyes and tried again to go to sleep. He felt so very drowsy.

THIRTEEN

*T*he wagon came around the last bend in the road and entered the lane that led through the huge old oak trees framing the large white two story house and prize winning flower garden. Ruth found great joy in the hard work required to maintain and improve the yard and flowers. Her roses were legendary and her gorgeous dahlia blooms were all the size of a large dinner plate. She had planned the layout of the garden so that it formed a simple but breathtakingly beautiful border around the old farm house. Oftentimes she would walk to the end of the lane and stand looking back just to take in the magnificence of the perfectly framed picture. From the lane you could see the end of the house with its dark gray slate roof and shuttered windows. The end profile revealed a large sweeping porch on your right, the front of the house, and on the back the summer kitchen dominated the picture. Each window was precisely framed by its dark green slatted wooden shutter that was every bit as functional as it was picturesque.

During the peak of the summer, when the ancient oak trees filled out to maximum foliage, the sides and the top of the house were framed in verdant hues, while the bottom of the house was perfectly completed by a patchwork of living color and texture from the flower garden. On this day, however, when the wagon rounded the bend the sight was distorted and anything but picture perfect.

Jeremiah pulled the horses up short, rubbed his eyes, shook his head and let out an audible moan. "What in the world?" Ruth was reluctant to move from where she was holding the now sleeping Isaiah. From where she was sitting, in back, on the floor of the wagon, she was unable to see the house and the distressing sight that had taken Jeremiah's breath away.

"What is it?" she asked, trying to see without disturbing the child who was lying in her arms.

"I honestly don't know," Jeremiah replied, "but somethin's not right!"

FOURTEEN

S teven wasn't really a bad boy, he just didn't know any better. The only good influence in his life came from the Miller family in general and Aaron in particular, but sometimes the fact that everything looked so perfect at the Miller farm just aggravated him.

"How kin' one family have so many good things happin' to 'em?" he often wondered. So, when he found it easy to lead Aaron astray it gave him a sense of power and control that otherwise he never experienced.

Steven had never had much to do with his father. It was mostly because his father was never around and had very little to do with his family. The man hated his wife, Ellen, and he hated the fact that he was expected to provide for her needs. When she got pregnant with Steven, he was livid. He blamed her for ruining his life and accused her of having the baby just so he would have to settle down.

One night, in a drunken rage, he broke up most of the furniture in the small Johnson family kitchen. Jorgen Johnson threatened his wife Ellen with a large hunting knife, broke out the windows in his home and fled into the night. It was days before he returned somewhat subdued and without a word of apology. He silently went about repairing the damage he had done. Ellen spent the whole time that he stayed around the homestead in fear but she dared not say a word. They co-existed, sharing the same household but not really having anything to do with each other. Ellen would prepare Jorgen's meals and leave them on the table. He would come in from the barn long enough to eat and then go out for the night. He stayed around long enough to stock the larder and then spoke the first word to her in months when he announced he was leaving, maybe for good. He always returned after a few months to get his clothes mended or replaced and on these visits he insisted Ellen be a wife to him. She was too afraid of him to tell him to stay away. Consequently he was an intermittent but destructive influence on Steven as he grew.

At first, Steven didn't understand much of the relationship between his father and his mother but later he understood more than he wanted to. When Jorgen did return he mostly stayed drunk but when he was sober he would lay around the house and curse and yell at anyone who got in his way. He even beat Ellen sometimes which used to send Steven into fits of rage that he knew he had to hide for fear of provoking his father even further. Steven knew he was not strong enough to stand up to his father and he was afraid of what Jorgen might do to his mom. So, life on the Johnson homestead was hard to endure and each time Jorgen left, Steven hoped that he wouldn't return. He even began to dream of terrible fates befalling his father while he traveled, and for some reason, this made him feel guilty.

Steven loved being around the Miller family. To him it was like a dream come true. Everyone respected each other and they treated each other as if they had value. But the tranquility of it all was too much and something inside Steven caused him to want to destroy what he could not have. His mother spoke of the Miller's as if they were angels of mercy and in fact Jeremiah had come to her rescue more than once when Jorgen was on one of his rampages. But, as Steven grew older, the fact that Jeremiah Miller had more control in the Johnson family than Steven did poured fuel on the already burning fire that was inside of him. So, he took every opportunity that he could to lead Aaron astray. The fact that it was so easy just served to encourage him.

FIFTEEN

Steven's heart nearly leaped out of his chest when Aaron first slipped on the cliff. He called out to him warning him not to let go of the ledge he gripped with his right hand. He had been in that same predicament himself when he was younger and first started climbing this cliff, but he was much more aggressive than Aaron and tight situations always made him fight harder. He remembered how scared he had been and how his sheer determination had given him the strength and fortitude to reach high and wide enough to secure him in the Bear's Hug avoiding the plummet that Aaron had just taken. Steven could see that Aaron was not tall enough, even if he had the strength necessary, to make it over the outcropping of rock and onto the easy section of Nightmare Cliff.

Why had he thought this was a good idea? Had he no notion of how dangerous this would be for a young boy who's desire to please his peers was stronger than his common sense? Steven prayed, perhaps for the first time in his life, but he didn't feel clumsy or self-conscious because the prayer came from deep within his heart, and he meant every word of it. "God, help him. I'm sorry."

As Steven had watched the clumsy ascent he saw Aaron reach for something solid but when he came away with nothing but air, gravity became the dominant force in the boy's life as he, at first, started sliding slowly then progressively faster. Steven didn't see how anyone could survive the fall that Aaron took and when Aaron came to a stop and didn't move there was no doubt left in Steven's mind that he had been mortally injured. He sank, involuntarily, to the ground and prayed harder—this time for himself.

"Oh God, help me. What do I do? I'm so scared. Don't let Aaron die. It ain't his fault. It's my fault." He hung his head and tears that had been building up for a life time came pouring out. Steven had completely forgotten about Alicia who was standing beside him as witness to this unbelievable sight. One of her friends was hanging lifelessly on the side of a cliff and the other was flat on the ground sobbing. She backed away, stunned by what she had witnessed and terrified by the state to which Steven had been reduced. Alicia turned and ran as fast and far as her legs would take her.

SIXTEEN

*R*uth had gently twisted her body around so that she could see the source of Jeremiah's bewilderment and when she finally caught sight of what remained of the flower garden she called *her pride and joy*, she wished she hadn't. A vast waste land dominated the landscape where once had been the most beautiful flowers and hedges. Shredded stems, petals and leaves that had once been prize winning rose bushes littered the yard. Laundry that had been clean and hanging on the clothesline soaking up the delightfully fresh and fragrant scent of the nearby flowers was now filthy and strewn about the yard. Her outdoor kitchen which she had spent a great deal of effort cleaning just hours ago, seemed to be covered with manure. What could possibly have happened? And there, looking pitiful in the middle of it all, sat Aaron!

Jeremiah reigned in the horses at the hitching post by the water trough, climbed down off the wagon and stood motionless, staring at the spectacle. He looked first from one end of the yard to the other and then at Aaron, sitting in the middle of a pile of laundry and contorted plant remains. Aaron had huge tears rolling down his face and a look of sheer terror in his eyes. To his left stood Mary, standing with her hands on her hips and a smirk on her face. Her apron and dress were soiled and her hair was no longer captured by the hair-combs. For a moment, Jeremiah thought she looked like her mother when she took that stance. Then his mind began to reconstruct the visible and invisible evidence at the scene of the crime.

Jeremiah slowly walked into the yard, surveying the damage. He could see that there had been a goat involved; the ground was still disturbed where Sam had obviously taken charge of the situation. By the size of the hoof prints the goat had to have been Billy. Slowly but clearly the entire scenario began to take shape as he visited each sight of destruction. But to Aaron's amazement, a small smile began to form on his father's lips and then, slowly, the smile began to grow until it became a grin and without warning the grin burst into a chuckle. By the time Ruth joined her husband they were both laughing an uncontrollable belly laugh. Mary and Aaron were in awe. What, about the carnage surrounding them, could possibly be laughable?

SEVENTEEN

S teven cried and cried and then cried some more. Years of pain and sorrow welled up inside of him. He had no idea what was happening, but he knew that the more he cried, the better he felt. Finally, exhausted, he lay quietly on the ground. He had been cleansed from years of abuse at the hands of someone he was supposed to look up to, to trust, to love. He finally knew the source of all his turmoil, the things that made him do what he did not want to do and to be what he did not want to be. He knew there was hope, even for him and with that he remembered Aaron. He quickly looked up but he couldn't immediately see any evidence of the young climber. He stood up and moved to a better vantage point and from there what he saw made him gasp. Forty feet in the air, suspended by some unseen force, was the only boy who had ever called him friend. Suddenly, he knew he had to get help no matter what the consequences. He ran and ran as he had never run before. For the first time in his life he had a reason to think of someone other than himself and he was glad.

It was about a mile, as the crow flies, from Nightmare Cliff to Tanger Creek, but by the time a boy went around steep embankments and thickets of trees too thick to crash through, the distance was almost doubled. When Steven arrived at the creek and the swimming hole nick named Big Hole he was terribly hot and sweaty. All afternoon he had been thinking of how wonderful the cool refreshing water was going to feel when the three friends finally made their way to the pool, but now he didn't even slow down long enough to get a drink. For a brief instant he thought about how he had used the reward of a dip in Big Hole to talk Aaron into daring the feat that had now, seemingly, taken his life. He wondered if Alicia had made it home by now; her house was much closer to the cliff than the Miller farm.

Even though his mind wandered his legs kept him going straight and did not slow down. Steven knew that Aaron's only hope, if he was still alive, was rescue before it got too dark and the sun was already at the top of the trees. From Tanger Creek it was another mile and a half to the Miller's but part of the distance was on a smooth road where Steven could make good time. He pushed on a little harder even though his side was splitting and his feet burned. He wanted more than anything to correct this terrible wrong that he had done. No matter how hard he ran the scenery seemed to pass in slow motion and now the sun seemed like it was on a direct unimpeded collision course with the earth. Nothing could stop it, and it was intent on its destination, moving faster by the moment.

Steven rounded the corner at the end of the lane as the Miller house came into view. It was such a beautiful sight, the house framed by lovely shades of natural color.

The Miller farm was nothing like his home. As much as his mother tried, there was never quite enough energy or money or time in a day to get everything done that the place required, and without a man around most of the time, the heavy things had to be hired out or left undone. Steven tried his best to do a man's work around the place but he had only just turned fifteen years old and there was much that he didn't have the skill or strength to do. Consequently the buildings were in disrepair, the fields produced less than they should and the house always seemed to need a new coat of paint. Ellen tried to plant flowers and keep the yard nice but after she finished the sewing that she took in on the side to support her and Steven, she didn't have the desire or will to tend what she had planted. Weeds grew up, paint peeled off the fence and shutters, and it all reminded her of the decaying state of her life. Steven felt guilty that he couldn't do more even though his ma never blamed him. It seemed, to those around Ellen, that she was always preparing for dark clouds and rain. She lived a life that was sure the storm was about to strike and, in fact, for her and Steven it was true. They never knew when Jorgen would return bringing with him rage, hatred, abuse and intolerance.

When Steven caught sight of the Miller house, in all its splendor, it caused him to stop. The beauty and tranquility stood as such a contrast to the traumatic news that he was obliged to deliver and it caught him by surprise. Here, in front of him, was everything that he lacked in a family and while he was envious at the same time he was resentful. He knew that if he walked away now he could bring a great blow of damage to the peaceful lives of the Miller's, but he also knew he could resist the temptation to cause more harm than had already been done.

Steven knew the only choice was to go, quickly and confess all, but how? What would they say? What would Jeremiah do? His experience with a father's wrath was at the end of a fist or a stick or a belt. In his heart he knew better of this man who was so gentle and yet so strong. The decision made, he sprinted the remaining distance to the yard, burst through the gate and yelled for help.

EIGHTEEN

*J*eremiah finished the evening chores, stored the grain buckets in the granary, closed the barn door and stood looking into the distance. He scratched his head. "Now where can that boy be? He knows he's supposed to be home for chores" he said, half to the animals looking at him through the fence and half to himself.

Jeremiah was upset about his son's obvious disregard for work that he knew had to be done but even more he was concerned for Aaron's welfare. This was unlike him. Certainly Aaron was prone to lose track of time and to get carried away with exploring, tree climbing and all those things so enticing to a young boy of twelve years but it was beginning to get dark and never had he missed all of the evening chores. Jeremiah slowly walked back to the house, reluctantly putting one foot in front of the other. 'What am I going tell Ruth?' he thought, when something caught his attention at the end of the lane. He stood still for a moment and squinted hard into the failing light. Nothing there. "Must have been a deer" he mumbled. His disappointment would have been obvious to anyone within earshot. He continued on up toward the house when he decided to go around the back side of the barn and make a final check of the new gate latch that Aaron had fixed.

Jeremiah rounded the corner of the barn, his thoughts intent on the possibilities of where Aaron might be and what he might be doing when he thought he heard someone yell. He stopped and listened. Yes, from the lane out in front of the house he definitely heard someone calling for help. Jeremiah ran, as a man with purpose, to the front of the barn and there in the lane — Steven? What in the world could Steven be doing here and what was he yelling about. Instantly Jeremiah's heart dropped. The look on the boy's face startled the strong Christian man. Here was terror as he had seldom, if ever, seen in his life and Jeremiah knew immediately that the source of Steven's alarm was Aaron.

Jeremiah rushed to Steven who was in tears kneeling on the ground by this time.

"What is it son?" Jeremiah fell to the ground beside the trembling blubbering boy.

Steven was usually moody, distant and untouchable although many times Jeremiah had tried to connect with him. Steven was not about to let any man inside his world because he knew what to expect from men. He had experienced it from his father and his opinion had been confirmed over and over by the words of his mother. But now, when Jeremiah took the boy's shoulders lifted his face and then hugged him to his chest, Steven did not resist. He needed all the compassion he could get, even if it was from a man who, as soon as he found out what had happened, would undoubtedly resort to physical violence.

Again Jeremiah asked the boy, "What is it son? What's happened to Aaron?"

The dam finally broke, "I din't mean it, I really din't. I just meant fer him ta' get scared, I promise," cried Steven in an almost unintelligible whimper.

"Where's Aaron, son? Where is he? Can you help him?"

By this time Ruth and Mary had come out of the house. They were both standing a ways off from the man and the cowering boy.

Ruth asked, "Do you need me to comfort him?"

"We're okay" was all Jeremiah said. He wrapped his arm around the boy and pulled him close to him. "Steven, you can help Aaron even now, but I need to know where he is—what kind of trouble he's in. God forgives you and so do Ruth and Mary and me, no matter what you've done. It's going to be all right son. You can trust me, you really can. I'm not going to hurt you."

Steven, bewildered, looked up into the face of Jeremiah and peace washed over him. His sobs began to lessen and his breaths came in more regular intervals as he trusted for the first time since he could remember.

"Aaron's up on Nightmare. He fell, he's hurt bad," Steven Paused, "if he's even alive" he confessed. He looked hard at Jeremiah once again and said, "It's my fault. I talked 'im into it. I hope he ain't dead. I prayed fer 'im—I ain't never prayed before."

Jeremiah sat back a little and withdrew his arm. Steven immediately flinched, he could already feel the inevitable blow but instead of striking Jeremiah took Steven's hands and said, "We're going to pray again, together right now." He looked over towards Ruth in the now dimming light and she and Mary came to them, knelt and they all joined hands.

"Dear God, hear our prayer." began Jeremiah. The heavens were opened and God reached down, one hand on the little circle at this very moment agreeing in prayer, and the other on a small damaged and terrified boy clinging to the side of Nightmare Cliff.

NINETEEN

*A*aron's legs were beginning to cramp. He pressed hard against the tiny ledge that stood between him and the edge of the cliff. His eyes closed and he slept for very short intervals but the sleep came fitfully and brought no real rest. As his head fell forward and his chin touched his chest his eyes opened with a start and terror, once again, invaded the short lived peace. The loss of blood and repeated surges of adrenaline had depleted Aaron's energy supply. He began to accept the circumstances that had overcome him but, somehow, bit by bit hope began to creep into his heart. After all that had happened he still lived! Maybe he could actually survive the night on this rock. As far as he knew his whereabouts were unknown to anyone except Alicia and Steven. The odds were that he would die here and his bones would be cleaned by the turkey vultures that would inevitably descend upon his carcass after his demise. The bare skull that still lay next to him was enough to convince him of this brutal fact and yet, beyond all odds, he hoped.

Aaron began to realize that his fate lay in the hands of the witnesses to the disaster. "Lord, forgive them for running away.

They didn't know what they were doing" he spoke to God who, even though he couldn't see Him, he had no doubt of His presence. Those words stuck in Aaron's mind and he played them over and over. 'They didn't know what they were doing. Forgive them, forgive them, forgive them.'

Aaron thought about Jesus hanging on a cross; as man, powerless to do anything to help Himself except to forgive the ones responsible for His pain and ultimate death. Aaron remembered his pa telling him that Jesus purchased life eternal for all men when He gave up His life. The concept of gaining by giving everything away perplexed Aaron. Somehow now, as he clung to the side of Nightmare Cliff, he began to understand what his father had tried to explain to him.

He felt real peace envelop him as he breathed the expression of forgiveness for those who had caused him this pain and what might possibly lead to his death. Even more overwhelming to him was the empathy that he felt for Steven. In an instant he saw the anguish of Steven's life. He could taste the bitter words of hate screamed by the boy's father and feel the sting of emotional violence that contorted Steven into the desperate soul that he was. And as Aaron envisioned all this his heart went out in a plea to God for forgiveness in Steven's life no matter what happened.

"God, I know Steven's goin' through a terrible time right now, help him see that You love him no matter what he's done. God, don't let him run from You all his life cause he needs yer help. Amen."

And with that, Aaron fell asleep, resting peacefully in the arms of his Lord. And God was pleased.

TWENTY

*J*eremiah grew up swimming in Big Hole and climbing on Nightmare Cliff, so he knew the way by heart, in fact he knew a short cut from his families homestead that few people were aware existed. However, it had been years since he followed this path and he wasn't even sure he could still find it. As he rode along his mind raced ahead of him. What would he find when he reached the cliff? He had made the climb up the famous rock face countless times and once even in the dead of night, but there had been a full moon and the face of the rock reflected moonlight as if it were the middle of the day. He remembered that climb well and how exhilarating it had felt to make that dangerous ascent in the brilliant moonlight.

Tonight, however, there was no moon. It was pitch black. The only light came from the lantern he carried in his hand. He could barely make out the main road that he was on and at times had to get down off the horse to make sure he was still on the right track. His inability to cover ground at the rate he desired caused him great frustration, but gave him ample opportunity to pray and believe God for the miracle he was convinced it would take to rescue his son.

Jeremiah sent Steven to Alicia's house for additional help. Ruth insisted on coming with him to the cliff but Jeremiah finally convinced her that her most valuable position was on her knees crying out to God on behalf of her son. Ruth knew the truth of what Jeremiah said but she desperately wanted to go to her son and comfort him. Reluctantly she agreed that she would stay behind with Mary and Isaiah praying as earnestly as they had ever prayed.

Jeremiah stood beside the side of the road, desperately searching his memory for details of the shortcut from the main road to Nightmare Cliff. He thought he remembered this big rock and the giant old oak tree with the limb big enough to hold an entire house but it looked so different by the light of the flickering flame. The years of absence and the increased underbrush caused him to question his judgment. He thanked the Lord for the moon that had finally risen, reflecting a clear and welcome light on the countryside.

The moon was on its waning cycle but still quite full and the bright light began to cast shadows across the path. Jeremiah had finally trusted his memory and the Lord's prompting and had left the main road on what he prayed was the short cut. The path was slow going, at first, but finally opened up allowing the horse to move freely and quickly. Jeremiah breathed another, "Thank you" to his creator and urged the horse on as fast as he could safely travel.

The surroundings were becoming more and more familiar. Memories returned of games of hide and seek, make-believe wars, imagined journeys to the west where many a bear was slain and many a river crossed in search of adventure. He spotted a branch that reminded him of a certain tree that he had climbed to the top. Images raced through his mind of skipping rocks on a section of the creek, building a big bonfire under the cliff where he and other boys spent countless nights on their own, free from the encumbrance of parents, chores and sisters.

The cliff—suddenly his mind became alert. He was near the climbing portion of the canyon wall but where would he find his son? Jeremiah began to wonder about his decision to send Steven for extra help. How would he find the exact spot where Aaron lay scared and injured?

Once again, Jeremiah relied on the Lord, "Father, You said to trust in You—ask in my name and you shall receive. Lord, that's what You said. Well, Father, I ask for my son. Show me where he is and how to get to him. Father I know that Ruth and Mary are agreeing with me right now. Father, God hear our prayer."

Angels in heaven wept to see Ruth, Mary and Jeremiah Miller pour out their hearts in this petition. They looked on the face of God to see what He would do on behalf of these faithful saints and God was moved to compassion. His mercy began to flow, to save and restore, knowing that in so doing His Son would be glorified in the testimony.

TWENTY ONE

*A*aron's dream contained many elements bordering on the real; the warm breath on his neck, the persistent nudging against his arm, the moisture on his cheek, the pawing on his arm. "Stop it Sam, I'm too tired to open my eyes." The sensations continued, "Sam, stop it. You're gettin' my face all wet. Come on, Sam, leave me alone." The dream refused to go away and now it was accompanied by a high pitched whine. Aaron's eyelids fluttered as he tried to open them, again the nudging and whining and now a wet nose in Aaron's ear. 'This dream is too real' he thought as he finally convinced his eyelids to open fully. There in his face was a big wet tongue and a cold black nose as Sam wagged her enthusiasm for her wakening master.

TWENTY TWO

Jeremiah tied the horse to a tree, took a rope off the saddle horn, placed it over his head and turned to face the cliff. He lifted the lantern toward the rock. The illumination was minimal. Jeremiah set the light down, walked a few feet away from it and let his eyes adjust to the moonlight. After a minute or two he realized that because of the reflecting light of the moon he had a much clearer overall view of the cliff without the use of the lantern so he left it where it was and walked along the base of the rock. He stopped and listened.

From a long way off came the lonesome hoot of a night owl hanging on the wind, searching for prey. The wind was picking up and the tops of the trees carried the rustled evidence of the movement. Clouds slid across the night sky, obscuring the beacon of the moon, now revealing its reflected light, then quickly dark again. In the distance Jeremiah heard a high pitched whistling sound that he recognized as Sam. He focused on the source of the sound but the wind carried it in circles and as it bounced off the rocks and trees it was impossible to determine its origin. 'Sam's here someplace' Jeremiah thought.

He whistled long and loud and waited. The wind answered with a gust in the tree tops. There—he heard it again. He was sure the sound had come from his left and up above him, but how—where could Sam be? He moved carefully along the path to the traditional climbing site. The brilliance of the moonlight enabled him to inspect the course that he had climbed so many times as a boy. The handholds were still there, the knobs of stone that formed perfect places to rest a foot, were unchanged by the passage of thirty years. Even the vines creeping down the side of the rock face were alive and flourishing but there was no sign or sound of Aaron or Sam.

Jeremiah whistled again for Sam and called Aaron's name but this time there was no response. In the distance, carried by the wind, came the sound of voices. Jeremiah turned and squinted into the dark forest, thankful for the assistance that was approaching Nightmare Cliff. As he peered into the darkness he could see several lanterns but he could no longer hear the accompanying voices. The lights were still quite a distance away so Jeremiah decided to turn his attention back to the cliff. He called once more, "Aaron, are you there? Can you hear me son? Aaron?"

A whining sound startled him. It was off to his left, possibly several yards from the only safe path up the cliff. The sound seemed to be thirty or forty feet above the ground, in the middle of the cliff. He was sure it was Sam but how could the dog be on the cliff?

Jeremiah searched his memory. There must be another way up, and then, in a flash of images, he remembered the land slide that had dislodged much of the overhanging embankment.

Jeremiah thought back to what seemed like an eternity ago on a bright spring day and the first climb of the season for his friends and him, but when they arrived they had discovered that the heavy rains of the spring had caused a landslide off to the left side of the traditional climbing sight. They enjoyed the exploration and newness of this recent development and had spent the day digging in the loose dirt and rocks but the thrill of climbing soon replaced their interest in the dirt pile.

Something about that landslide lodged in Jeremiah's mind. He moved along the bottom of the cliff to an outcropping of granite, the trees and underbrush grew right up to the face of the cliff so he had to squeeze around the protruding rock. The underbrush was so thick and dense that he was forced to push the tree limbs aside in order to get through the tangle. As he made his way through he let go of a branch and it sprang back and slapped across his face knocking his hat off and scratching his cheek. He stumbled around the rock and in the darkness fell over a bank of dirt overgrown with weeds and vines.

Just as he remembered, the landslide spilled to the bottom of the cliff embankment and on into the underbrush at the base of the cliff. Each year the heavy spring rains and run off from the loose bank above added soil, rock and other organic material to the pile creating a steep ramp now high enough that the top was beyond Jeremiah's vision. He tested the soil which, the last time he had climbed on it, had been loose but now, over years of accumulation, was densely packed.

He called again for Aaron and Sam, "Son, are you there? Sam, where are you girl?" This time, Jeremiah was greeted by a short loud bark and then he saw movement. Suddenly a few loose stones came rolling down the steep ramp and then a small cascade of dirt followed. Jeremiah quickly climbed down to the bottom of the slope as dirt started sliding down on him. He jumped back to avoid being covered. In the dark he could see an object at what appeared to be the top of the ramp coming slowly down, now faster, now sliding and rolling and now at his feet wagging its tail and barking. Sam jumped up on Jeremiah, barked again and then in a flurry of activity and cascading dirt scurried up the steep ramp and on to a small ledge that led to the right and out of sight.

"Wait for me, girl" Jeremiah called to Sam. "I'm comin' Aaron" he cried, "hang on son, I'm comin'." Jeremiah scrambled up as high as he could but the higher he got the looser the dirt was and it kept sliding out from under him. He couldn't quite reach the ledge of rock that Sam was standing on, wagging her tail encouraging as much speed as possible.

Jeremiah slid down the dirt pile to the bottom. Sam barked her disapproval and disappeared down the ledge. Jeremiah looked to see if the lights were any closer but the underbrush obscured his vision. He looked at the slope, said a quick prayer and scrambled up the dirt again. This time he got high enough to reach the ledge with his hands. He clawed at the rock as the dirt gave way under his feet. With every ounce of strength and determination that he could muster he clung to the rock as the earth crumbled beneath him. His toes searched for footholds and finally his right foot was successful. Now he gripped with both hands and his foot to the side of the cliff. He pulled himself up with all his might and was able to hoist his body up onto the ledge where he had last seen Sam.

The ledge was quite wide, as far as he could see, but then it disappeared around the face of the outcropping of rock that Jeremiah had negotiated on the ground and through the bushes. Jeremiah called again, "Aaron, are you up here?" Silence. "Sam, where are you? Where's Aaron, girl?" Sam responded with an urgent bark. "Okay, girl, I'm coming." Jeremiah moved along the face of the cliff, a little too recklessly, and stumbled around a rock shoulder into pitch black. He slipped on some loose rock, fell backward and frantically reached for something to hang on to. His hand felt a vine which he gripped tightly but it came out of its shallow soil and his momentum and the force of gravity carried him to the edge of the ledge. Somehow, by shear will, he stayed on the ledge even though he fell to his knees, ripping his britches and the flesh underneath.

In the total darkness he thanked God that he hadn't fallen further. He stayed motionless for a moment catching his breath and vowing not to be so reckless and to move with a little more caution. He would be no help to his son if he ended up at the bottom of this cliff.

God in heaven heard the prayers of this man and was pleased. He moved His hand and the clouds dispersed, the sky was clear and the moon shone with a new intensity.

From this vantage point Jeremiah could see the lanterns of Steven and Alicia's father and brothers. They were still far enough away that they looked like fireflies. Jeremiah knelt on the ledge fascinated by the way the lights seemed to go here and there, first one way and now another. 'They must be lost in the dark cause they sure don't seem to be getting any closer' he thought.

A wet tongue and cold nose brought him back to the mission at hand. Sam whimpered as if to say, "You're almost there, don't stop now."

Jeremiah looked at this faithful companion, "Okay girl, lead me to Aaron." Jeremiah was ready for whatever was to come.

Sam turned around on the ledge and disappeared around the protruding face of the rock outcropping. Jeremiah stood up slowly making sure of his footing. The moon shone its light clearly on the path and he began to follow Sam. He called again, "Aaron, where are you son? I'm here, I'm comin' for ya', hang on son."

TWENTY THREE

J eremiah and Ruth looked at each other as they laughed and the emotion that had been building in them since they had first seen Isaiah poured out in an overwhelming flood. God was so good and His plan was without flaw. They knew this in an instant and their faith was increased. At the moment when they thought the world had collapsed around them and things couldn't possibly get worse, they had walked upon a scene that was so incredibly wrong they could only laugh.

God has a way, when things look the darkest, to reveal the truth of what we hold dear in our lives. If we hold a flower bed in reverence He shows us how quickly it fades, 'one day beautiful, the next thrown in the fire.' If we hold our families so dear that they come between us and God's will, He permanently changes that which we had built our life around. And now, for the Miller family, life changed, transformed and became new.

Ruth laughed at the mess that now represented her pride and joy, not because it was funny, but rather that she had once held it with such pride. Jeremiah laughed at the mess, not because it amused him, but because he had once measured his success as a Christian man by the order in his life and his model family. Here, in the course of an afternoon, God had managed to turn their world upside down in such a way that most people would fall crushed under the weight of the changes. However, Ruth and Jeremiah chose to view the events of this day as a beginning and they determined they would never again place limits on what they would allow God to do in their lives.

Ruth broke away from her husband and began to stroll through the yard. "These flowers needed a good pruning. You know, I never really liked that bush over there, it looks much better here. Now this hedge is going to need some work but I think it can be salvaged. What do you think, Mary?"

Mary's smile slipped from her face. Her mouth was wide open in disbelief! The delight she expected to receive at the punishment of her brother was beginning to lose its flavor. Then her face took on a very puzzled look as she noticed a little face peering over the seat of the wagon just a few yards away. Ruth followed her gaze to see Isaiah, staring at the mystery before him.

"Aaron, Mary, come over here, we want you to meet someone." Jeremiah ushered the kids over to the wagon where Ruth had gathered Isaiah into her arms. Aaron looked at Mary who looked back at him then they both stared at Isaiah.

"Meet Isaiah. Your new baby brother"
"What's he doing here?" Mary asked.

"And what happened to his face?" chimed in Aaron.

Jeremiah and Ruth had told the kids of the fire that had taken Isaiah's parent's lives, but they hadn't told the horrific details of the fire and how little Isaiah had been horribly scared.

They also hadn't shared the dilemma of who was going to assume the responsibility of raising the little survivor.

Jeremiah explained, "Isaiah needs a new family and your mother and I believe God has chosen us to be that family."

"But why does he stare like that? Can't he see?" Aaron wanted to know.

"He looks so strange" agreed Mary with a mixed air of disgust and unbelief.

Ruth wrapped a blanket around Isaiah and carried him into the house. Jeremiah took this opportunity to talk to Aaron and Mary.

"You remember Joanna told us about the awful fire that killed my brother Peter and his wife Maria? Well, Joanna told your mother and me that their son Isaiah had also been burned but we never imagined the extent of the scars on his face. When we met him at the train station this morning, this is what we found. Jonathan said he's been like this since the fire. He hasn't said a word or made any kind of sound—won't look at anyone or make any contact with anyone and he just stares. Nobody knows what he sees."

"I know this is going to be hard on us all and we'll all have to make sacrifices but he needs us. There's nowhere else for him to go. Your mother and I thought the best thing to do was just bring him home. I know we usually talk about things first in this family, but the truth is, there isn't much to talk about when you know it's what God wants you to do." Jeremiah paused, "Do you understand?"

"I guess so pa" Aaron reassured his father, not too convincingly.

"Well, you could a' told us first." Mary said. "Where's he gonna' sleep? We only have three bedrooms?"

"Now that's a good question, Mary" Jeremiah responded. "This is where we need to ask for your help." He turned to his son. "We figured the best thing is for him to stay with Aaron until I can add another room on to the house. What do you think son?"

"I don't see why he has to be in my room!" Aaron said a little too quickly. Then he remembered Billy, the yard and the predicament he was in and said, "I mean, sure pa. He can stay in my room."

Jeremiah looked at Aaron, a little surprised, then he said "Good son, we all have to make sacrifices now. He'll need a place that he can call his own." Jeremiah put his arm around his son and began to walk towards the side of the house, "Mary, why don't you go in and see if you can help your mother. I'd like to talk privately to Aaron about what happened to the yard and a few other things like—responsibility."

Mary smiled a big devilish smile at her brother and sauntered off to the house, full of self-righteousness. 'Yes' she thought. 'There is a God!'

Aaron had mistakenly thought that by his eager agreement to Pa's suggestions about Isaiah and the living arrangements that he might escape giving an explanation about the condition of the yard and how it came to be in this state. And, if he escaped the explanation, he might even avoid the inevitable punishment that was bound to accompany the story.

But, as usual, Pa didn't forget. Jeremiah once again examined the yard and thought to himself, 'If nothing else, this ought to be quite the story' as Aaron slowly began to pour out his confession. At this moment Aaron was about to learn the old saying, *'truth is the most powerful defense.'*

TWENTY FOUR

*A*aron's eyes opened and his mind began to replay the events of the day. He didn't want to believe all that he had been through. He wanted to close his eyes and sleep and then—in the morning—open them to see the pattern of the paper on his bedroom walls. He hadn't really noticed it before but now he could describe it in detail. Little things that had seemed of no importance before now stuck out in his mind; like the way the rooster crowed his wake up alarm each morning and the way the sunlight streamed into his room and danced across the floor. Aaron found it fascinating to watch the different path the light took as the seasons changed and as he thought about the sun light, he noticed the shadows on the rock beside him. How they danced and played along the crevice of the shelf of rock right above his head. Light, so bright that it cast a shadow—at night?

Aaron's body, while weak from the trauma, strenuous activity and lack of food and water, was no longer in shock. His mind, for the first time in hours, functioned properly and began to set his senses in order. His eyes began to focus; his hearing became clear, he could feel the cool breeze on his skin and even though the pain was still very real, he was in stable condition. Had he really dreamed of Sam licking his face and nudging his arm? That seemed ages ago. Aaron decided to check his injuries and began to adjust his position so that he was more exposed to the moonlight now streaming so brightly.

His shoulder, somehow during his final fall, had been set back into place so although it was still very painful and tender it was no longer dislocated. The blood that he so clearly remembered on his hands, arms and face seemed to be, for the most part, gone. Aaron began to question himself and his memory when Sam poked her head around the corner and rushed into her master's arms. "Sam! It was you. I thought I was dreamin'.'"

At this moment, the fact that Aaron was on the side of a cliff and his dog was wagging her tail beside him and licking his face didn't seem impossible. He was just happy to have her with him. Slowly it dawned on him—"What are ya' doin' here girl? How'd ya' get up here?" Sam barked and Aaron heard a muffled voice come from somewhere in the distance. At this moment he noticed the lights dancing in the blackness of space out in front of him. "I saw those lights before, didn't I?"

Again, Aaron heard something. This time it seemed closer and more familiar. He called out, "I'm up here—help me!"

Jeremiah heard the sound he had been praying for, "Thank you God!" and he yelled again. "Aaron." There was no response but now he was sure his son was here and he was alive and it was only a matter of time before they would be down off this rock and home safe and sound.

"Aaron—can you hear me?" he yelled as he moved toward the hump in the side of the cliff. He moved carefully now, he didn't want to lose his footing but he was desperate to find his son who he knew was so close.

"Pa—is that you, Pa?" Aaron was sure he had heard his father's voice. Sam barked confirmation and Aaron's spirits soared. He tried to stand up but was too weak so he sat back down. "Pa—I'm here—I'm okay. Can ya' hear me?"

"Aaron I hear you. I'm just comin' around the face of the rock son. Are you okay? Are ya' hurt?" Jeremiah's progress around the protrusion of rock was extremely slow and the anticipation of seeing his son was excruciating. But he was determined not to make a mistake. He moved further, almost rounding the rock, now he could see the other side and his heart dropped as he saw the end of the ridge of rock that he was using as a path. "Where are you—Aaron?"

During the fall, when Aaron had grabbed the root of the tree stump, the action had slowed his fall enough to keep him from catapulting off the side of the cliff. In doing so, the direction of his momentum had changed drastically enough to veer him several yards off of the normal climbing route. He had actually ended up around the far side of the nose of Nightmare Cliff, a place that very few climbers ever ventured simply because of its inaccessibility from the ground. Ultimately he had ended up coming to rest in a crevice where separate rock formations joined together forming a small cave. The ledge that Jeremiah followed led directly into the crevice but did not go on beyond. When he first came around the rock he saw only a bare sheer cliff in front of him. How could this be? Where was his son? The moon was bright enough that it cast deep shadows in the folds of the rock so Jeremiah continued to move slowly. "Aaron—are you here somewhere? I can't see you."

"Pa, I'm here. I can see you, Pa. Right in front of ya'." Aaron spoke and Sam agreed with a bark.

"Son—I can't see you, but I'm gonna come as far as I can on this ledge. Are you hurt? Can you stand up?"

"I think my shoulders broke or somethin', I don't feel so good—Pa, I'm scared. I know ya' told me a hundred times not to try ta' be somethin' I ain't. Pa—I'm so sorry." The tears that had previously been denied now flowed freely down Aaron's cheeks. Gravity pulled them to the rock cradling this young helpless boy and they colored the stone where they fell leaving stained evidence of his repentance.

Jeremiah's heart broke. His son lay broken, on the side of a sheer cliff, and yet his principal concern was whether he had disappointed his father. "Aaron—don't even think about that right now. I'm going to get you off this rock, that's what we need to concentrate on right now—nothin' else. Okay, son? I love you"

Jeremiah heard the sobs of his son but the sound he heard was emotion brought on by love, relief and thankfulness, not fear. At that moment, the moon's reflective light seemed to grow in intensity. The reflection on the rock face dimmed and something almost like a beacon of light penetrated the darkness of the little crevice. There, not ten feet in front of Jeremiah, was the huddled form of his son. Jeremiah's heart leapt into his throat as he recognized Aaron's shape for what it was. The young boy was tucked into the tiny cave of rock—his foot braced against a small ledge of rock serving as a hedge of protection between him and the steep drop below. At his side was Sam, tail wagging wildly. Jeremiah quickly scanned the cliff face directly above the little fold in the rock. There was no visible way that Aaron could fall from above and land in this fold of rock, yet somehow, there he was—battered and torn but alive and Jeremiah knew that this was a miracle of God!

The ledge between Aaron and his father was wide and level and he had no trouble covering the last few steps between him and his son. He knelt down in the lee of the rock and cradled Aaron in his arms. They both wept for joy at their reunion.

"Can you move your arm son?"

"Not so good, Pa. It hurts a lot."

"Okay—that's okay. I'll pick you up. It's gonna' hurt—but I've gotta' get you off this cliff." Jeremiah put his arm under his son and began to lift him gently into his arms. He stood up slowly and carefully as he steadied himself against the rock wall. As soon as he felt confident, he began to retrace his steps along the edge of Nightmare Cliff, moving slowly and surely along in the steady moonlight that illuminated his way.

The two could now hear voices at the base of the cliff.

"We're up here" Jeremiah yelled. "Over on the far side of the hump." The lanterns weren't visible so he knew the rescue party couldn't see Aaron and him.

"Jeremiah—is that you?" came the voice of Jim Langely, Alicia's father.

"Yeah, Jim, it's me. You'll have to go around—through the brush to get to where we'll be coming down. I'm gonna' need some help from the ground," directed Jeremiah. "Aaron's okay! He's pretty beat up but he's gonna' be okay. Steven, are you there, son?"

"Yes sir—I'm here Mr. Miller. We came, fast as we could—got lost in the dark—couldn't find the path. Sorry" Steven yelled from the bottom of the cliff. "I know where ya' are, we're comin' Aaron, we're comin'."

"Sorry it took so long Jeremiah," apologized Jim, "I used ta' know the way but it's been so many years since I been to the Cliff more times than I care to think about." Jim began cutting a way through the thick underbrush around the chin of the face of rock as Jeremiah worked his way slowly along the narrow ledge, his back against the rock wall.

Aaron lay still in his father's arms, afraid to look down let alone make any movement that might cause a stumble. He prayed for strength for his father and courage for him.

"I know what ya' mean Jim—it's been a long time, huh. Thank ya' for comin' so late at night" Jeremiah hollered down to the men at the bottom of the rock.

"Ain't nothin'. You'd do the same fer me an' mine. I'm just glad I can help, now let's get ya' both offa' that rock," answered Jim.

The rescuers below set their lanterns on each side of the steep slope rising to within eight feet of the narrow ledge. Jeremiah rounded the hump in the rock and stepped from the soft gentle moonlight into the bright light from the lanterns which momentarily blinded him. His foot stepped too far forward into thin air throwing off his center of gravity. He pitched forward—the weight of the boy in his arms pulling him even further away from the solid rock. Jeremiah realized there was nothing to hold on to or to keep them from sailing off the side of the cliff; so with a quick prayer he stopped fighting the force of nature that wanted to pull him to the ground and let his weight drop down to the ledge. His bottom side landed hard on the rock but instead of recoiling from the shock he absorbed it and tried to become one with the rock. Just as quickly as he had begun the fall it ended with him sitting on the ledge, his son still safely in his arms. "Thank you, Lord" he breathed.

"Take it easy up there, Jeremiah. I don't want ta' be diggin' no graves tonight. Ya like ta' scare me ta' death," Jim tried to lighten the tension.

"You've got a point there, Jim." Jeremiah took a deep breath to calm his nerves. "I'm gonna have to lower Aaron down to you 'cause the soil's real lose right there. I'll tie this rope around him—under his arms and slide him down the rock right to where you're standing."

Aaron groaned as the rope tightened around his chest and squeezed into his under arms. He determined to make no further sound for he was almost on the ground that, not long ago, he had been sure he would never touch again while he was alive. The fact was, that in spite of his pain, he couldn't be more relieved. He felt his legs being grabbed from below and then the pressure being released from the rope. The next thing he knew he was lying on the ground; looking past the light of the lantern into the night sky, thinking how beautiful and bright the stars shone even in the bright light of the moon. Life seemed sweeter, more real, less demanding, he was alive and safe and on solid ground.

Aaron was lost in thought when he noticed, out of the corner of his eye, a face staring at him. It was Steven! Steven took a step closer into Aaron's line of sight—knelt down and leaned right up to him. "I'm sorry, Aaron. I'm really sorry." But before Aaron could respond Steven was up and running past Jeremiah coming down the bottom of the dirt slope. Steven pushed past the man and burst through the newly cut path in the brush which grabbed his shirt! Steven ripped away from the grip of the bush, tearing cloth and skin in the process! In his anguish he was not even aware of the torn shirt or the pain from the scratches on his arms and side or the blood now flowing freely. His intent was to get far away—as fast as he could.

Jeremiah followed right behind him. When they reached the other side of the bushes and the rock face, Jeremiah grabbed Steven's arm.

"Let me go—let me go!" cried Steven as he spun around, fists pounding the air. "Don't touch me! I ain't no good fer nothing. Leave me alone, I ain't worth nothin'!" Jeremiah pulled the boy around so that they were facing each other and now the raining blows from Steven's fists began to make contact with Jeremiah's arms and chest, but instead of stopping the attack he absorbed it.

"It's okay son—go ahead—get it all out. It's okay—let it go. Let it go." Jeremiah received the frustration and pain stored up inside of this child from years of neglect and abuse and slowly the blows softened and the tears became more powerful. He pulled the boy to his chest and hugged him tight, "I love you son. God loves you."

Abruptly Steven pulled away, "How can you say that? If God loves me how come he gave me such a mean pa?"

"God doesn't make people mean," Jeremiah assured him.

"Well—if he's God how come he don't do somethin' about it? How come he lets my ma get beat?" Steven pulled free from Jeremiah's grip and turned taking a few steps. "Sometimes—I think things about my pa—it scares me what I think about, what I might do. But then I think, I can't stand ta' see him doin' what he does. I wish he'd never come back. I wish he was dead." Steven finally said out loud what he had been thinking for so many years.

"Sometimes bad things happen to good people. Steven listen to me—there's a devil in this world and his whole purpose is to destroy. And he likes destroying people more than anything else. He delights to do it in the worst way he can think of. You and your ma don't deserve to be treated that way."

"But why's He let it happen? He's God ain't He?"

"God lets people make their own choice and if the devil gets a hold of them—he tells them all kinds of lies. A lot of people believe those lies—but it doesn't matter what you've done or what has been done to you, God still loves you. He'll make a way for you to get free from the devil." Jeremiah paused to see if any of this was getting through to Steven. After a moment he continued, "God always loved you and always will. That's why Jesus died on the cross for us, Steven. I know you've heard me talk about this before, but right now it's real important that you understand that God loves you and wants to save you from all that's happened to you." He paused again. "I know things have happened to you that should never happen to anyone and God knows how bad you hurt inside. He wants to help you but you've got to let Him."

"I want that—real bad—but I'm scared. What if it don't work? What if Pa comes back and what if" he paused, "what if I do somethin' terrible? I'm so scared—I just want ta' run."

Jeremiah touched the boys shoulder and Steven turned around to face him. Jeremiah saw a fifteen year old boy who had already lived a full life time and his heart broke.

"Son, this is a very important moment. Look deep in your heart—you know God's waiting just outside the door. He's knocking son. He wants in so bad. You know He does. This would be a good time to trust Him cause you've got nothin' to lose, do you?"

"Ya' gotta' *have* somethin' before ya' got somethin' ta' lose." Steven spoke wisdom beyond his years.

"Well, with a word you can have everything God has to offer. What do you say?" Jeremiah asked.

"Yeah, I want that Mr. Miller. I really need that."

A ripple washed over the angels standing guard over this scene being played in the moonlight at the bottom of a cliff that Satan had intended for evil and God had used for good.

TWENTY FIVE

*R*uth and Mary watched as Jeremiah rode down the lane. Steven had gone on to Alicia's house to get help from her father and brother.

Ruth stared into the dark night thinking about the twists and turns her family's life had taken recently: first the awful fire, then the addition of Isaiah to the family which stopped all the dreams she and Jeremiah had of moving west to the frontier, and now—she didn't even want to think about the possibilities of what lie before Jeremiah when he arrived at Nightmare Cliff. Where was God in all this? What was He doing besides stretching the faith of this little family?

Mary stood silently beside her, more focused on Ruth than on the situation at hand. She had rarely seen her mother like this: moody, silent, unwilling to share what she was thinking. Usually, Mary could count on talking about everything with Ma. They were often like two sisters confiding their deepest heart-felt secrets to each other.

Growing up in such a rural setting, with very few close neighbors and even fewer close friends, had the result of bringing a mother and a daughter into the deepest friendship. It was not as if Ruth was not a mother to Mary, for she had no problem in that area, but their relationship was more than just mother and daughter—they were best friends.

Mary knew that the events of the last few weeks had changed her ma. She was less like a sister now and more like a mother. Rarely did she have time to talk to Mary about all the things they used to discuss. It seemed like Isaiah consumed all her thoughts and time. More than once Mary had come excitedly into the kitchen where her mother was working, hoping to talk girl talk, but her mother was too busy. She would say something like, "Shh, your little brother might wake up." or "I was just thinking and praying about your little brother." Mary began to grow resentful of the time that Isaiah occupied in her mother's life and she hated when Ruth called him, *her little brother.*

Once Mary even said, "He's not my brother." The look on Ruth's face startled Mary who quickly ran outside, but instead of her mother chasing after her and scolding her as she expected, Ruth said nothing. In fact, Ruth never called Isaiah, *her little brother* again, which of course, made Mary feel guilty.

Mary studied her mother in the lantern light; the way her hair curled down the side of her face and streamed down her back, the way she stood so tall and straight, looking so strong. She thought how beautiful her mother was and how she loved her so very much and she was sorry that she had not been more help to her during this difficult time.

"Mother, I—I owe you an apology."

"Mary, you…" Ruth tried to stop her but Mary continued.

"No, mother, I need to say I'm sorry for how I've been lately," she said quickly before she lost her nerve.

"I know you are dear. Thank you for the apology and now it's my turn," Ruth responded.

"No, you have nothing to be sorry for," Mary said quickly, "I'm the one who has been so nasty,"

Ruth paused for a moment letting Mary's words settle. "I really don't blame you," she said finally. "Not that it makes it right, but it has been very difficult for you with Isaiah here." Ruth spoke to herself as much as to her daughter. "Mary, it wasn't right for us to just bring him home without talking to you and Aaron first."

"But it was. You were following God. What else could you do?" Mary assured her.

"It makes me very glad to hear you say that, Mary. You've grown into a fine young woman and I am so proud of you." Ruth began to confide to Mary, "I had no idea what it would mean to bring that little child into this house—how difficult it would be. At the time it just seemed like the thing God would have us do, the best solution." She thought about how her life had changed since Isaiah came into the house, "God must know something I don't because there are times when I just cry. I don't know what to do for him other than to love him and hold him. I thank God that at least he allows me to do that. I don't know what I'd do if I couldn't even hold him. But that seems to be all that I can do; feed him, keep him clean and love him." She began to cry softly. "And now I'm thinking of him when my own flesh and blood may be at the bottom of a cliff dying or dead." She began crying harder and Mary held her.

"Mama, don't cry. Aaron will be fine. You know that. We have to pray, God will save him. You know He will."

Over the top of her mother's head Mary saw a little face peaking around the door frame. She gave her mother a squeeze and got up and went to Isaiah who retreated inside the door as she came.

"It's okay Isaiah, Mama's okay." Mary knelt down in front of the door and was drawn into the eyes that peered at her from around the corner of the door frame. "What does he see when he stares like that? No one should ever have to witness such things, such horror, especially a little child." She hesitated then held out her arms to him. "We have to pray for Aaron. He's in trouble and we must ask God to help him." Isaiah came towards her slowly as she continued to wait, arms outstretched. His head was down now, his eyes on the floor. Then he lifted his face and the dark piercing stare penetrated her soul for the first time. Tears dropped from her cheeks to darken the wood floor and her arms reached for him. He did not resist and Ruth, who had crossed over to the two of them, knelt down beside them and began to pray. Isaiah stood in the center of the hug as the two women prayed in earnest for Aaron and Jeremiah.

They prayed there on the porch until Isaiah curled up in Mary's arms. Ruth and Mary continued to petition God and to thank Him for the angels that He had assigned to this important task. They prayed for strength and wisdom for Jeremiah, strength and courage for Aaron and thanked God that Steven had been brave enough to come for help. They felt compelled to pray that Steven would come to know Jesus as his Savior. They prayed for unity and love in the family and that God's will be done on earth as it is in heaven. Finally, they sang some hymns. Isaiah slept through it all, a look of peace on his face.

When they were done Mary carried the tiny Isaiah up to Aaron's room and placed him under the covers of his own makeshift bed. The little boy was fast asleep and God smiled and nodded in approval.

TWENTY SIX

Jeremiah stared into the deep of the night as he rode along—his arm wrapped around his son. The steady rhythmic gate of the horse and the rocking motion in the saddle gently lulled Aaron to sleep.

The night, etched by the amazing events that had taken place, had an almost mystical feel. Jeremiah mulled over all that had happened and thought 'Each day brings a mystery crafted by God and our destiny is molded by how we unravel that mystery. It seems if we try to comprehend every moment and place value on it, we miss the bigger picture and see only the pieces of a puzzle. Much like missing the forest for all the trees.' He mused. 'Who would ever have suspected that through this would-be tragedy, God could gain a new child for His kingdom?' Jeremiah chuckled a little and then laughed out loud. 'What an awesome God we serve' he thought.

Aaron stirred in the saddle, lifted his head for a moment, opened his eyes and then let them close—his chin resting against his chest. He was exhausted both physically and emotionally and sleep came easily to him knowing he was safe in his father's arms. Jeremiah paid no attention to the lane or where they were or how they progressed. He trusted the memory of his horse, Nellie, who had pulled a wagon down this lane more times than he could remember. He knew her main interest was home and the reward of grain she would receive at the end of her work. The night sky was now crystal clear and every breath of air seemed so fresh. Jeremiah drew the air deep into his lungs and slowly exhaled. He thanked God for answered prayer, his life and his family and the many blessings that God had bestowed upon them.

Nellie plodded along, her head hanging down until she rounded a corner then without warning, she whinnied loud and strong signaling to her friends in the barn to move over, she was almost home. Sam, trotting alongside them, echoed her sentiment with a bark.

Jeremiah woke from his revelry knowing instantly the meaning of the disturbance. He reigned in Nellie who thought this might be a good time to break into a trot. 'Whoa, girl. Let's walk now—got an injured passenger on board." The horse relinquished but continued to toss her head eager for the end of this long and unusual day.

Jeremiah could now see the lanterns in the windows of the house, their flickering light offering a warm welcome. He squinted to see if anyone was waiting on the porch. He was eager to share the success of the night with his wife and daughter but the porch was empty.

Nellie whinnied again, Sam barked and the door of the house opened quickly as Mary, followed closely by Ruth, came running out on to the porch and down the steps into the yard. They came through the yard gate as Nellie stopped short in front of the fence.

There was great rejoicing that night after Aaron's wounds were tended to and he was tucked safely into bed. He was so exhausted that he declined to even eat before he fell fast asleep. Ruth and Mary stayed at his bedside praying and rejoicing, giving God the glory, while Jeremiah cleaned himself up. In the kitchen, while Ruth and Mary prepared food for the hungry rescuer, Jeremiah faithfully recounted all that had happened. They made him repeat many parts, some, just so they could hear them again and others because they could hardly believe how God had worked out one thing after another. The story of Steven's salvation was of particular interest and Jeremiah ended up retelling that part three times. There were great hugs and kisses and many tears of joy and amazement. Finally the hour and the day's excitement began to take their toll so with a long hug they bid each other good night and went off to bed.

As Jeremiah settled in under the covers he felt warm, comfortable, and safe. Ruth sat at her dressing table brushing her hair and staring into the mirror without really focusing on the image in front of her. After several minutes she turned to Jeremiah and said, "We should have talked with Mary and Aaron before we brought Isaiah home."

"I know." Jeremiah agreed.

"Did we do the right thing bringing him here," she asked?

"Yes. We did the right thing," he reassured her.

"And everything's going to be okay?" her question probed.

He propped himself up on the pillow, "Honey, everything will be alright. We don't know what the future will bring or what will happen. But as long as we continue to trust and believe God, everything will work out, even with Isaiah."

She turned to face him, "Thank you! I needed that reassurance. Now go to sleep."

"I was trying to," he teased and lay back down. Within minutes he was snoring peacefully.

Ruth pulled the covers up on his arms and slipped quietly from the room. Her first stop was Mary's room. The door was open a crack so she peaked inside. There, kneeling next to the bed was her daughter. Ruth marveled at how life situations shape and mold a person. Here, before her, was her firstborn, a beautiful girl who had somehow become a woman right before her eyes. Ruth wondered at all God had done in Mary's life just in the last few months. She said a short prayer thanking God for such a daughter and friend.

Next she moved to Aaron's room to check on him and Isaiah. She walked softly to the partially opened door not wanting to waken her recovering son. The room was dark and the form in the bed didn't look quite the way she expected. Concerned that she had missed something in her diagnosis of Aaron's injuries she stole quietly into the room. She tip-toed over to the sleeping form and let her eyes gradually adjust to the light. She stared at the bed in disbelief. What she saw took her breath away. Just then a quiet sound startled her. She turned to see Jeremiah in the doorway. He began to say something but she put her finger to her lips and motioned for him to join her. There, curled up next to Aaron was Isaiah. The boys slept soundly, Aaron's arm tucked carefully under Isaiah's shoulders. They looked peaceful, serene, as if they belonged there—like two long-lost brothers finally reunited.

THE END

Dear Reader,

We hope you have enjoyed this short novel **Nightmare Cliff**. This story of a small portion of a young boy's journey to adulthood was written to help encourage the theatre of your mind. Situations and images have been presented for you, the reader, to be able to first imagine the story and second to prompt dialog both internally and externally.

Aaron Miller is faced with choices not too far removed from the choices that every young person faces. There are three areas of discussion that we would like to encourage by using the following methods:

- **Language Builders**—colloquialisms, idioms, slang and other vocabulary challenges
- **Decision Builders**—how decisions form our perspective and develop character through the consequences of our actions
- **Faith Builders**—God's principles and character as it relates to us

We hope you enjoy this process and think of it as an extension of what you have already enjoyed in **Nightmare Cliff** rather than a tedious exercise. This process can be even more fun in a group setting, so have your friends read the book and discuss the questions together.

May you be blessed as you complete this challenge.

Marty Hogen
marty@crosspurposeproductions.com

'Nightmare Cliff' Discussion and Reflection Questions

Language Builders:

1. What does, '**...better part of a day...**' mean? (first part Chapter 2)
2. What are '**britches**'? (middle chapter 2)
3. What does '**skimpin**' mean? (middle chapter 2)
4. What does '**zealous**' mean? (middle chapter 2)
5. What does it mean when it says that Aaron's lunch made a surprise visit? How is that personification? (end chapter 3)
6. What does the term, '**women's work**' mean? (middle chapter 3)
7. What does '**unbeknownst**' mean? (chapter 5)
8. What is the metaphor, '**silent wooden sentry**' referring to? (chapter 5)
9. What does the colloquialism, '**setting things to rights**' mean? (middle chapter 7)
10. What does the phrase '**none the worse for wear**' mean? (end chapter 8)

11. What does the term **'ebb and flow'** mean? (first portion of Chapter 9)

12. What does the idiom, **'hit the road'** mean? (end chapter 9)

13. What is a **colloquialism**?

14. When something that is not alive is given living and human characteristics it is called **personification**. Find something personified in chapter 3. What is it? Describe some of those aspects of personification?

15. A **metaphor** is a comparison of two things that are not related to each other. They help the reader understand something that they might not be familiar with by comparing the unfamiliar thing with a familiar thing. Find a metaphor in the story—write the two things being compared with each other.

Decision Builders:

1. Discuss Pa's philosophy of work as described in the first part of chapter 2.

2. Do you think children should have chores? Do you have chores? What are they? Why is it important to have chores?

3. Have you ever concocted a story with the motive to deceive someone? What do we commonly call that? Why does it seem easy to do this sometimes?

4. Why do you think Steven wanted to destroy the Miller family? What is the emotion that he displays by this type of thought and action?

5. Do you think Steven deserved to be forgiven?

6. Discuss Aaron's reaction to his parents return. (end chapter 10)

7. Have you ever done something that you knew you shouldn't have done? Did you get into trouble? How did you feel before you got in trouble?

8. Discuss the word "**consequences**" associated with '**letting father down**'. (beginning chapter 9)

9. What does it mean to '**please your peers**'? (first part chapter 15)

10. What is the '**waning cycle**' of the moon? (chapter 20)

11. What does the term, "**a night owl hanging on the wind**" mean? (beginning chapter 22)

12. What does the term, "**truth is the most powerful defense**" mean? Pg. 68

Faith Builder Discussions:

(You will need a bible for these questions.)

1. Read **Galatians 4:17-19**. How does this relate to the fence building story?

2. What does 'faith' mean to you? Why does it involve something you can't see? If you can see it does it take 'faith' to believe in it?

3. Read **Psalm 19:1-6**. What is being described by the Psalmist? Discuss this imagery. Can you make up another description about something observable similar to this?

4. Read **Psalm 31**. Discuss what it means to be a Psalm 31 woman. How does this compare to the derogatory statement, '**women's work**' made earlier in the book?

5. Read **Mark 12:41-44**. Discuss this story. What does it mean to you? How does it relate to *Nightmare Cliff*? Discuss the concept of a 'wilderness journey'.

6. Read **Romans 8:28**. Now read **Genesis 50:20**. Compare these two scriptures. How do they relate to Jeremiah's struggle and thoughts about this situation?

7. Read **Romans 7:18-25**. How does this scripture describe the struggle that we all face every day? How does this play into our ability and desire to do the right thing? Can we overcome our sinful nature? How does the Apostle Paul end chapter 7? How can this encourage us?

8. Read **1 Corinthians 10:13**. Here the Apostle Paul is describing what happens when we ask Jesus to be the Lord of our life. How does that relate to the previous question of **Romans 7**?

9. Discuss Steven's prayer. Pg. 40. Do you think it felt real to you? What did you like about it? What didn't you like? How did it make you feel when the Miller's forgave him? Do you have anyone that you have not forgiven?

10. Read **Matthew 6:14-16** and **Luke 6:36-38**. What does this say about forgiveness? How important is it? Is it easy for you to forgive? What if the person has not said they are sorry or shown any signs of being sorry for what they did?

11. Do you think God has forgiven you for sins you have committed?

CPSIA information can be obtained at www.ICGtesting.com
Printed in the USA
BVOW02s0254170913

331358BV00002B/5/P